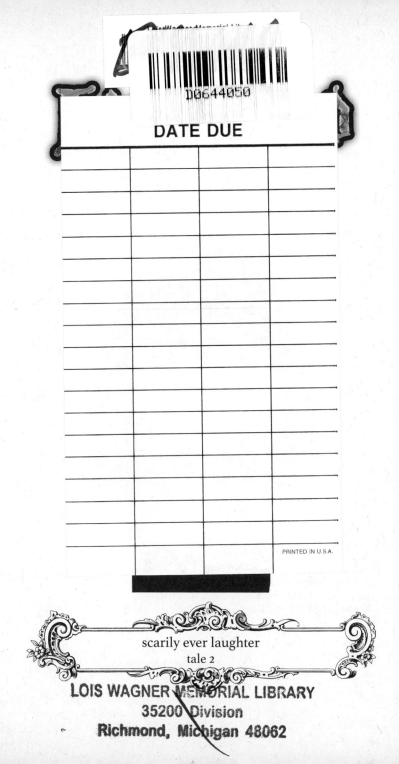

scarily ever laughter
tale 2

For information on subsidiary rights, please contact the publisher at rights@jollyfishpress.com. For information, write us at:
Jolly Fish Press, PO Box 1773, Provo, UT 84603-1773.

Printed in the United States of America

THIS TITLE IS ALSO AVAILABLE AS AN EBOOK.

Library of Congress Cataloging-in-Publication Data

Borst, Amie, 1975- author.
 Little Dead Riding Hood / Amie Borst, Bethanie Borst ; illustrated by Rachael Caringella.
    pages cm. -- (Scarily ever laughter ; tale 2)
  ISBN 978-1-939967-89-3 (paperback)
[1. Vampires--Fiction. 2. Friendship--Fiction. 3. Middle schools--Fiction. 4. Schools--Fiction.] I. Borst, Bethanie, 2000- author. II. Caringella, Rachael, 1988- illustrator. III. Title.
 PZ7.B6484965Li 2014
 [Fic]--dc23

                    2014021216

10 9 8 7 6 5 4 3 2

$18.99 4/17

Also by Amie & Bethanie Borst:

Cinderskella

scarily ever laughter
tale 2

Amie Borst
Bethanie Borst

illustrated by
Rachael Caringella

JOLLY
FISH
PRESS
PROVO, UTAH

Chapter 1

You know things are going to suck when you're the new kid. But when you're the new kid and a vampire . . . well, then it totally bites.

From the beginning, I could tell things would be sucktastic. But not in a good, vampire-blood-sucking way.

Mort and I shuffled wordlessly into the car, my bag jampacked with stuff she thought I'd need for yet another first day adventure. If you could call it that. More like torture if you asked me.

My jeans pinched at my thighs and I wanted nothing more than to rip them off and put on my black lace, high-collared mourning dress. Anything that made me feel more like myself.

Mort drove in silence, the hiss from the engine louder than usual. I waited for her to recite the rules. I could almost hear her.

"Remember the rules, Scarlet. No sneaking out for a midnight snack, no biting the other kids at school, and no showing off with your centuries-old, smarty-pants education."

"Fine, Mort. Of course not, Mort. I'd never do that, Mort. And show off? Who me? Never happen."

Mort's simple little trill of a laugh—the one that tells me she loves me, despite all we've been through—rang in my ears.

I laughed out loud and snapped back into reality. Mort shot me a look like she thought I was crazy. But I bet she would have laughed, too, if she'd heard the conversation.

A feeling of sadness swept over me. I longed for Mort's normal lecture and her confession of loving me with all her unbeating heart. I would have even been willing to let her embarrass me in public with VDAs (Vampire Displays of Affection—you know, all that huggy-kissy stuff vampire parents like to do to their little suckers).

Mort pulled the car up to the curb, her eyes fixed straight ahead.

The silence pounded in my ears as I reached for the door handle. I stepped out onto the sidewalk, leaving the door ajar. "Well . . . Thanks . . . I guess . . ." I stammered, feeling even more nervous about another new school because of Mort's new attitude. "I guess I'll see you after school."

Mort grunted, then snapped her head toward me, our eyes meeting for the first time. "This is our last move, Scarlet." Her pale skin flamed with color as she clenched her teeth. "You mess up this time, and Drac and I will have no choice . . ." She lifted her nose and sniffed the air suddenly. Maybe the yummy smell of my classmates tempted her too much. Mort swallowed hard like she wanted to say more, but didn't.

She didn't have to. My undead heart skipped a beat and my limbs grew numb. Mort and Drac were going to send me to the Underworld. If a vampire can't make it work topside, that's the only place for us to go. The thought of meeting Mr. Death again gave me shivers, and I couldn't bear it. My lips moved in objection but nothing came out.

I jumped out of the way as Mort leaned across the seat and slammed the door shut. Her tires squealed as she took off out of the parking lot like a bat out of . . . well . . . you know where. In fact, I think it's safe to say she left skid marks on the pavement.

I stared at Mort's car as it chugged along, sputtering down the road, steam hissing from the engine and puffs of smoke escaping the tailpipe.

And by car I mean a jalopy of a vehicle, somewhat resembling a form of transportation on four wheels. Why she hadn't upgraded to something more modern is beyond me. It was probably because of my dad, Drac. He said the twenties were roaring, and I guess he just couldn't accept the idea of leaving that decade behind. Thankfully he had agreed to give up his Brook Brothers suit for this move. If only I could make the zoot suit disappear, too.

But Mort . . . she didn't even blow me a kiss. No goodbye. No nothing.

I stood on the curb and gawked. First at Mort's car, which was completely out of sight in less than T-minus ten . . . nine . . . yup. Gone.

Without tears in my eyes, because I was not crying—not because of Mort, and certainly not about starting at a new school again—I gawked at the building. It was the same as all the other schools I'd attended. Same boring red brick façade with fingerprint-smudged windows. Same double-door entry that tried to look inviting beneath layers of tacky-colored paint. Plus, I could smell my classmates. Their rich blood made my mouth water and stomach gurgle.

I scanned the building, looking for a broken window. I'd have a better chance of surviving (and so would my classmates) if I knew what to expect. All the other schools had one, and . . . yup. There it was. At the far left corner, second story. I bet it was the science lab where some kid thought he was funny combining chemicals that didn't get along very well. From the looks of it, he nearly blew the school to smithereens.

If the broken window and science lab stuff were true, then there would certainly be a pecking order here.

You know, every school has one.

The star athlete who uses sports as a crutch because he can't pull off good grades.

Miss Popularity who thinks she's important because no matter how hard she tries, she never measures up at home.

A teacher's pet who pretends to be perfect because deep inside she fears failure.

A class clown who hides behind a disability like ADHD.

And the school bully who's really mean because he has no self-esteem from being bullied at home.

This may seem a little grown-up and insightful for a kid, but trust me. I've been around long enough to know this stuff is true. And I can usually find them in the first week, sometimes sooner.

Which makes forming friendships even harder. As if being a middle-school vampire wasn't hard enough, there were rules. Some of them I learned the hard way.

VAMPIRE RULE #29

Obey vampire rule number one. Friends don't like being a meal. It kind of puts a damper on the whole friendship thing, even if they were only so-called friends to begin with.

As far as fitting in with my peers, well that never happens. Ever. At my old school they just called me a goth freak. Whatever that is. Mort said it was probably on account of wearing combat boots with dark, old fashioned dresses with buckles and black lace all the time. That's why she'd dumped a heap of new clothes on my casket; she said they might help me fit in better. I'd had a hard time parting with my high-collared mourning dress, but at least she let me keep my purple Dr. Martins, my favorite pair of combat boots. I'd picked them up in Seattle in the early 90s when grunge was all the rage.

Memories and emotions flooded my undead body.

I missed the Victorian era. It was my favorite time period. I'd enjoyed some of my best meals then, back when blood wasn't so polluted. Things weren't the same when we became vegetarians.

I pushed those thoughts deep into my belly, which still gurgled like a witch's cauldron with last night's dinner. Skunk, in case you were wondering.

I'd just have to suck it up.

Except I couldn't help thinking about Mort and why she took off so fast. Why didn't she bother to say goodbye? Or recite the rules? Or kiss me? Not that I wanted her to kiss me. That's lame. Every kid hates that. Still, I didn't know what was eating her. Maybe the skunk wasn't sitting well with her, either. She always said it left a bad taste in her mouth.

Focus, Scarlet. I let out a sigh and read the marquee. Last week was the Spring Fling and report cards would be distributed next week. Good thing I didn't have to worry about any of that.

It took a minute for me to notice the school name. Sure it was displayed over the entrance like some sort of crowning glory, but it's not like I really paid attention. As usual, it was a boring name of some old man who the town thought did something interesting a really long time ago. If it had been done today it would probably result in an indefinite prison sentence.

"Charles Perrault Middle School," I whispered under my breath. "Charles Perrault? Where have I heard that name before?"

"Fairy tales," a voice said from behind.

"Whoa!" I cried, spinning around. To my amazement, there stood a girl with blonde hair and large, blue eyes. And I'm pretty sure she was talking to me, but I couldn't be sure. None of my peers had ever talked to me . . . well, except when they were calling me names . . . or saying something like, "Oh, please, no!" as they ran in the opposite direction when I tried to suck the life out of them. But there she was, staring. At me.

Chapter 2

As I stared back at her, my lips revealing too many teeth, I remembered a rule.

VAMPIRE RULE #101
Keep your smiling to a minimum or you will look like a deranged freak.

My smile quickly faded and I ducked behind my long, shaggy bangs, hiding my face from view. As I did, something dawned on me. Why hadn't I heard—or more importantly, smelled—her approach? My senses were usually right on. Being a vampire and all, I can smell blood from a mile away. It was probably one of my best qualities. For some reason, I really wasn't at my best. Mort's behavior probably threw me off. My stomach bubbled and popped. Or maybe I had acquired her disdain for skunk. "I mean, what? What did you say?"

"Fairy tales. Charles Perrault, he wrote loads of them." She held out a boney-looking hand and I reluctantly placed mine in hers. "Cindy," she said, glancing over my shoulder. "So, new in town?"

"Um, yeah. Sure." Even though I'd been through the new-kid scenario a gazillion times (usually ignored, teased, or stared at) I was caught off guard by this girl. "I mean, yes. I am. We just moved in . . . down the street." It was hard looking people in the eye, so I fixed my eyes at my hand in hers. When I realized she might feel my cold, undead skin I blinked and pulled away. I didn't want her to know my secret so soon. I certainly didn't need any alarms going off already. I couldn't upset Mort and Drac. There's no way I'd allow them to send me to the Underworld.

"Well, great! I'll show you around." Cindy grabbed for my hand again, but I tucked it behind my back before she could reach it. As she moved closer, that's when I realized something seriously different about this girl. Her smell. Not the normal iron-rich smell that comes from all living, breathing humans pumping yummy, sweet blood through their veins. No, hers was more of a dull, earthy fragrance, like dirt and autumn leaves. It reminded me of Halloween and cemeteries and other scary things like that. But oddly, I wasn't scared of her.

"So, sixth grade or seventh?" She eyed me curiously, sizing me up. "You look too young for eighth."

"You think so?" My voice cracked with a laugh. If she only knew! I'd completed middle school more times than I cared to count. Plus I am older than dirt. Literally.

"Sorry . . . I just meant that . . ." She tucked a strand of blonde hair behind her ear, and the same earthy scent floated in the air between us. "That you look young."

She probably thought I was short, too, since I only came up to her shoulder, but she was too nice to admit it. "It's okay. I get that a lot." Actually, it was a first. But that was probably because no one ever talked to me.

Her cheeks flushed pink. "I'm in sixth," she volunteered. She didn't need to know I'd completed sixth grade for the umpteenth time. She also didn't need to know I'd been instructed to enroll in seventh. "Me too," I said before I could stop myself.

Mort and Drac would be infuriated when they found out. After all, no one disobeyed General Drac. My throat got tight as I remembered the Underworld. Remembered Mr. Death. If I messed up and someone found out my vampire secret, they'd have no choice but to send me away.

"Seriously?" Cindy beamed. "Well, that's the best news I've heard today." Her strange scent wafted through the air again, punching my nostrils like the heavyweight champion of the year.

This girl was just too much. I couldn't pass up more time with her. Between her chipper personality and the weird smell, I just had to find out more about her. Besides, the old suckers would get over it when they realized my super-quick thinking would allow us to stay an extra year longer. Or so I hoped.

"Yeah, seriously." I tried to smile, but it was more of a catawampus, awkward grin.

"You okay?" she asked.

"Just . . . nervous . . . you know?" C'mon! You can do this! "It's my first time in middle school." Good job! That was perfect.

"You mean you didn't transfer from a middle school?"

What?! For devil's sake this girl is good! My hands dripped with sweat and my undead heart gave one good thump in my chest. "Uh . . . My last school was a private school . . . kindergarten through sixth." Phew! That was a close one!

"Oh, right. Well, if I can tell you a secret, I was nervous my first day in middle school too. It's not as horrible as you think it is. Except for Mr. G. Petto. He's kind of a bald-headed freak."

She tilted her head like she was picturing him in her mind or something. "He likes to carve wood into puppets. Sometimes, if you sneak up to his house and spy on him late at night, you can see him dancing around . . ." Cindy looked at me horrified, eyes bulging. "I mean . . . It's too bad you didn't get here last week. You just missed the Spring Fling." She twisted a lock of hair around her finger.

Even though I'd seen the notice on the marquee, I still

acted surprised. "A dance?" At this point, I'd heard them all: Spring Fling, Fall Formal, Sock Hop and Winter Waltz.

"Yeah. It was the best dance ever!" Cindy beamed again, but she looked more like she was hiding something important. "So, why'd you move in the middle of the school year?"

You can do this. "Dad." I sighed like I wanted sympathy just so she wouldn't think I was weird. "He's in the army." It was so nice to have someone talk to me for once instead of running away, but interacting with my peers felt so weird. And exhausting.

"That must be tough," Cindy said. "Or exciting. Guess it depends on how you look at it. You know . . . the power of an attitude adjustment and all."

VAMPIRE RULE #102
Note to self: Make note about attitude adjustments.

"Attitude adjustment?" That was a new one.

"Yeah, kinda like looking at something bad as something maybe not so bad . . . like maybe it's a good thing bad things happen. Sometimes it's not as awful as you might think. Know what I mean?"

Strangely, I understood perfectly what she meant. "I think I know exactly what you mean." Nothing's ever as bad as I think it might be. So I'm not sure why I still felt upset by Mort's little drop-and-run. She must have had a good reason for it, right? Unless the Underworld was her reason, then . . . GULP. "Yeah, the moving isn't bad at all. I've gotten used to it. Er—I've had an attitude adjustment." I showed her my cheerful side, even though I knew I'd never fit in no matter how many new schools I went to.

Cindy laughed. Something about it told me somehow, she might have experience with that, too—looking at things differently, and having a positive attitude, that is.

And somehow, I thought I would really like this earthy-smelling girl.

Maybe because, for starters, I had no desire to eat her.

Chapter 3

As soon as I stepped into the school, a new smell barreled into me like a wrecking ball. I wondered why I hadn't noticed it before. It made me want to vomit.

Saliva and fur. And manure. Like a farm. But worse. At least with farm animals you can smell their tasty blood—which, for a vampire, always masks the smell of everything yucky.

This stench almost masked the beautiful fragrance of the hundreds of sweet-blooded middle-schoolers. Only one thing on the planet had a smell like that: dog.

Wet, nasty, disgusting dog.

I hate dogs.

I reached a hand up to plug my nose but Cindy grabbed it, dragging me to the main office. Normally I hate having people touch my cold, undead skin, but I didn't really mind because her earthy fragrance helped cover up the foul odor floating around the school. A little bit, anyway.

I couldn't help but notice that this Cindy girl was really into that touchy, feely thing. Personally, I preferred the feeling of sinking my fangs into a human.

But we vampires have rules about those sorts of things.

VAMPIRE RULE #1

If a vampire bites a human they have two choices: Make them into a tasty meal, or turn them into a vampire. Simple!

VAMPIRE RULE #2

Don't bite humans. It makes rule number one so much easier.

But she didn't need to know that—just like she didn't need to know why my skin felt ice cold. I actually wondered why she didn't say anything about it whenever she grabbed my hand. I figured she politely pretended not to notice. Kind of like how I didn't say anything about her strange smell. Either that or she was just weird. Or maybe both.

Cindy opened the door to the main office. "You probably need your schedule, right?"

"Schedule?" My eyes felt like they would pop out of my head. Why hadn't I thought this through better? And why did I feel so off-kilter? I should have been able to handle all this simple stuff—but Mort usually took care of all that boring paperwork stuff. How would I do this on my own?

I thought about my decision to enroll in sixth grade. Maybe Mort wouldn't be angry that I'd messed up. After all, if she really wanted me in seventh grade, she would have enrolled me herself, instead of trusting me to do it.

"For your classes." Cindy combed her fingers through her long, blonde hair. Her smell wafted through the air.

"Oh, right."

Cindy tapped on the silver bell situated on the counter. The receptionist, who snoozed silently, bolted upright and pushed her rolling chair away from the desk. She stood up, tucking a pen behind her ear, quickly hidden behind waves of blonde hair. She gracefully approached, her head held high as if she were balancing invisible books. "We have a 'no hat' policy here at Charles Perrault." The top pearl button on her cardigan had come loose and it dangled by a single thread, jingling back and forth as she spoke.

My eyes fixated on the button—the lady's one imperfection.

Cindy cleared her throat, making me jump. "What?"

"Take off your hat," Cindy whispered behind her cupped hand.

"Oh, right. No hats." Bummer. Hats protect me from sunlight, so I don't sparkle and glitter. Kidding. You don't actually believe that do you? I burn easily. Fair skin.

"It's a cute hat," Cindy said, touching the brim.

"It's not a hat. It's a fedora." I removed it, my hair cascading down my shoulders, bangs falling into my eyes.

"Oh. Well it makes you look adorable."

I brushed my bangs out of the way. But they just fell back into my eyes a moment later. I had the most uncooperative hair ever. "I prefer fadorable."

Cindy chuckled. "Fadorable it is then."

"Name," the lady interrupted. "Please," she added with a sugary sweetness.

Didn't she just hear that I'm Fadorable?

"Scarlet." Cindy elbowed me in the ribs.

I peered at her through my dark bangs. "What?"

"Her name is Scarlet, Ms. Lily." Cindy sighed. Did she seem frustrated? "Scarlet. . .?"

"Small," I said. "My name is Scarlet Small."

Ms. Lily rifled through a stack of papers on the desk, apparently looking for my schedule. Obviously she wouldn't find it since Mort hadn't done her part to enroll me in school. When she didn't find what she looked for, she let out a funny little sigh and went to her computer. "Strange," she said, smoothing her golden locks. "I don't have you in the system."

I gulped. "You don't?" I batted my eyes sheepishly. I used my vampire mind-control powers to smooth things over, my forehead wrinkling with concentration.

VAMPIRE RULE #108
Vampires don't have mind-control powers.

Ms. Lily shook her head. "All right, just fill out this form. We'll have your parents sign it later. Sixth grade, right?"

I nodded.

She printed off a schedule and handed it to me.

"Thanks." Before I could fold the paper and slip it into my binder, Cindy tore it away.

"Hey! Would you look at that?" she squealed. "We have all the same classes!"

Things just got interesting.

Chapter 4

"I'll show you around. First stop: the girls' room."
Cindy handed back my schedule. She marched us
through the office doors, up two sets of stairs, past
a row of lockers, and around a corner to the bathroom.

She bounded into the room like she was part of a sting
operation. Or like Miss Popularity announcing her arrival.
She didn't quite seem like the Miss Popularity type though.
Weird. Usually I excelled at this stuff. Boy, I was really out
of whack.

I stood in the doorway. No way would I go into the bathroom with other people around. There was a chance they'd
see my non-reflection in the mirror, and that would blow
my cover.

"You coming?" Cindy's call echoed from inside the girls'
room.

"Nah." I shrugged, lips pursed, trying to look too cool for a mirror check. Even though Cindy couldn't see me, other kids could. I needed to look believable. I couldn't let on so soon about my vampire status, no matter how badly I wanted to hang out with earthy-smelling girl. "I think I'll just try to find my locker."

"Well, hold up. I'll help you." She bounced back out of the bathroom and hooked her arm with mine.

We headed off together in the direction of a set of blue lockers, but Cindy stopped short when she saw another girl standing there. "Chickey monkey!" she said gleefully.

"Chickeroo!" The girl hugged Cindy, giggling.

I gaped at them both, unable to relate to all the bubbly-girliness.

"Oh. I'm sorry Scarlet." Cindy brushed a strand of hair behind her ear. "This is my BFF, Sarah."

"BFF?"

The two girls laughed out loud.

"BFF. It means Best Friend Forever."

Before I could respond, Cindy grabbed my schedule again, which had both my locker number and its combination printed at the top of the page near my name. Locker number 666—last one in the row, and it was mine. She knelt down and twisted the dial in a fury of boney fingers and skin. The door popped open revealing an empty locker. "There you go!"

I brushed my bangs out of my eyes. Again. "Thanks."

Cindy inched out of the way while Sarah stood two doors down, books in her arms. I knelt down, and began unloading my supplies.

Cindy opened locker number 665. Right next to mine. The door squeaked open, and the ceiling lights reflected off a shiny surface. I turned away and quickly shielded my eyes.

"What's wrong?" Cindy asked.

I peeked through my fingers allowing my eyes to dart from her face to the locker door.

"It's just a mirror." She plucked it from the door and handed it to me.

I pushed it away. "I have a massive zilch!"

"Zilch?" Cindy furrowed her brow. "What's a zilch?"

Think fast, Scarlet. Zi . . . Zil . . . No wait! I remember. It's Zit! That's it! "I mean zit! I have a massive zit! See?" I pointed to my chin. No wonder I never fit in. I couldn't even remember a simple word. "I can't bear to look at it." Tipping backward, I put my arm dramatically to my forehead in despair. I could be such a drama queen. Besides, it always worked for the actresses in Mort's favorite movies, why not for me?

Cindy laughed. "Well, I don't see anything. But I know how you feel." She put the mirror back on the door. "I think I have some cream in here. . .somewhere." Cindy fished around in her locker. In the distance, I noticed two boys swaggering toward us. They were nearly the same height, though the one with shaggy blonde hair had about an inch on his wavy brown-haired counterpart.

The brown-haired boy tapped Cindy on the shoulder. She whirled around and flashed a smile. "Ethan!"

The boy named Ethan hugged her. But I could tell he really wanted to plant a friendly little kiss on her cheek. Cindy blushed. He turned back and when his eyes met mine they narrowed. It made me feel squirmy. I didn't like it one bit. So I diverted my eyes only to see the shaggy-haired boy leaning against a locker, one leg crossed in front of the other as Sarah swooned pathetically. Gross.

"Oh. Sorry. Let me introduce you to—" Cindy caught me staring.

"Scarlet." I glared at Ethan, gritting my teeth. This boy rubbed me the wrong way and, for the death of me, I couldn't figure out why.

"Everything all right?" Cindy asked, catching the death-stares Ethan and I shot at each other.

Blend in, Scarlet. Be calm. Do your best. I seemed to hear Mort's voice in my head.

"Scarlet Small," I said trying to be calm, cool and collected, just like Mort would want.

"Ethan. Ethan McCallister." He reached out his hand to shake mine. "And that's my brother, Hunter." He jabbed a thumb over his shoulder, pointing at the shaggy-haired boy who sauntered down the hall with Sarah at his side. Something about this whole encounter made me queasy. My senses were usually pretty good at detecting when something was amiss. Already I had weird vibes, so I knew I needed to be on alert.

I shook his warm, sweaty hand. As I did, the nasty, foul smell that I'd smelled the moment I entered the school suddenly punched my nostrils. It was worse than the stench of a gazillion dogs who'd gone for a swim in a slimy, algae-filled pond. And I'm not even exaggerating.

I nearly keeled over. And that's pretty bad since I'm already dead.

"Oh gol-ly. Who brought the dog to school?" I tried really hard not to gag. But the smell felt like a weight on the back of my tongue, urging bile up from my stomach in some sort of Olympic game. The bile, my tongue, and that rancid smell were all competing for the gold medal. "I mean really. I think I might puke!"

Ethan rubbed his ears like my words pained him. Did he have really big ears, or was it just my imagination?

Ethan's gaze darted from me to Cindy.

Cindy looked like she would burst into tears at any second. Her eyebrows knitted together in the center of her forehead, and her mouth formed an upside down crescent. And Ethan, well, Ethan . . . he looked constipated as he shot his gaze at me. What big eyes he had!

Normally I don't mind when people look at me—I mean, being a vampire and all, I'm used to being noticed, no matter how hard I try to blend in. Then, all of a sudden, Ethan's blue eyes narrowed into almond-shaped slits of glowing green.

But that wasn't all. His lip curled up until I could see his sparkling white teeth.

My, what big teeth he had!

He snarled.

A loud, dog-like snapping growl of a sound!

My undead heart leapt in my chest. If I didn't know better, I'd almost swear it started beating again.

I got that squirmy feeling in the pit of my stomach. The same squirmy feeling I usually get when I'm near my mortal enemy. The mortal enemy to every vampire.

That's what made me realize it wasn't a dog I smelled. No, it was, without a doubt, the boy standing in front of me. People can't be dogs, now can they? But they can be worse. Much worse.

All of that added up to a really icky, horrible, miserable realization.

Ethan McCallister was a good-for-nothing, mouth-frothing, butt-licking, rabies-infected, flea-infested, animal-disguised-as-a-human werewolf!

Chapter 5

I gasped, filling my lungs with too much air, making me cough hard. My chest ached—either from raunchy dog-smelling air or from regret. I couldn't believe I'd enrolled in sixth grade! What was I thinking? If I'd enrolled in seventh grade like I had been instructed, I wouldn't have to deal with a werewolf as a classmate. How would I ever stay out of trouble? I was doomed to an eternity in the Underworld with Mr. Death forcing me to labor in The All-Seeing Fields.

Cindy must have sensed the tension because she grabbed my hand. Again. She dragged me to class like a puppy. Maybe she was used to that. You know, since she and Ethan seemed to have a "thing." Werewolves need direction, or else they get caught up scratching at their fleas or licking their butts or some other gross thing like that. But I was not a werewolf. And I certainly didn't need direction. Still, I let her do it since that's probably what friends do. Not that I would know since I'd never had a friend. Well, not since becoming a vampire, anyway.

After sitting through a bunch of boring classes, Cindy dragged me to the least boring part of the day—lunch. I love lunch.

For one, it's the part of middle school where social lines are drawn. That line identifies the pops from the rejects, the band geeks from the jocks, the artsy kids from the cheerleaders. At every school, my curiosity always gets the better of me, even if I know I'll be seated with the rejects.

For another, I was hungry.

I could barely control myself around all those sweet-smelling humans. My mouth watered.

Within minutes Sarah and Hunter joined us, Ethan sauntering close behind. My stomach lurched. Stupid dog-boy. I stuffed a crunchy, grease-coated French fry into my mouth.

Cafeteria food is so gross. You'd think after all this time of being a vampire, I'd be used to it, but somehow it seems to get worse every year. If I didn't have to eat it to fit in, I'd stick with my vegetarian vampire diet. Plus, if I didn't put food in my mouth, I'd be turning all of my classmates into a tasty snack.

Ethan plopped his tray of food on the table, glaring straight at me. If I didn't know any better I would have thought dog-boy presented a challenge. Dogs are like that, especially if they feel threatened. But that was silly. He couldn't have known my vampire status, so there was no reason for him to be threatened.

He stabbed his fork into a French fry, and swirled the fry in a mound of ketchup. He chomped down, letting the red ick drip from the corner of his mouth.

That's something I will never understand. If tomatoes are a fruit, then ketchup is a smoothie. I can't imagine putting a smoothie on my fries! That's just gross. But give me a Bloody Tom—my all-time favorite blend of vegetable juice and O positive—and I will gulp it down like there's no tomorrow! It's a special vampire brand; our version of V8.

"Want some?" Ethan shoved his food-filled fork in my face, waving it in a circle. Hunter snorted while Sarah grimaced uncomfortably as they watched Ethan taunt me. "Its sooooo good."

"No. Keep it away from me!"

Everyone sitting at the table stared at me like I was some sort of freak show.

"It's just ketchup," Cindy said.

Oh no. I needed to blend in, look normal. "I mean, YUMMMM. I can't wait to have some of those delicious fries covered in ketchup." I was so proud of myself. It didn't sound rehearsed at all! Well . . . if unrehearsed sounded like a bad actor quoting even worse lines . . . Oh who was I kidding? My lines sounded totally scripted.

Mort was wrong. New clothes wouldn't change anything. I would never be good at fitting in.

"Great!" Cindy reached for a handful of ketchup packets, tore them open and emptied them onto my tray.

I propped my elbow on the table and rested my face against my hand. "Fangtastic." My hair fell into my eyes shielding me from the awkward gazes of everyone.

"What?" Ethan leaned forward. "What did you just say?"

Shoot! I didn't just say that! "I said, fantastic. You know, FANNNN-tastic . . . because I just looooove French fries covered in ketchup."

"Then have at it!" Hunter said as he tossed me a handful of ketchup packets. He was quickly becoming as annoying as his brother. Did werewolf genes run in the family? Nah. Everyone knows you've got to be bitten.

Sarah giggled as she sipped her chocolate milk.

Cindy snorted. "You're a hoot." She emptied another packet on my fries. "Bone appetite."

"You mean bon appetit," I said in my best French accent.

"Sure. That's exactly what I meant." Cindy flashed Ethan a smile.

I lifted a ketchup-smothered fry to my lips. Just think of it as blood. The fry was inches from my mouth, the sickening smell of tomatoes mixed with high-fructose corn syrup invading my nostrils. It's not that much different than a Bloody Tom. About to chomp into it the bell rang.

Saved by the bell! The glorious bell.

No one seemed to pay any attention at that point because they all dumped their trays in the trash and hurried off to their next class.

Lucky for me, right after lunch, it was time for a nap. You know, also known as math class. I slept through the lecture (probably not the best way to make a good first impression), waking in a puddle of my own drool when the bell rang. I rushed outside, thankful I'd survived the first day at my new middle school.

I kept an eye out for Mort's antique car with the big wagon-styled wheels and hissing radiator at the bus loop. While I waited, I watched all the delicious-smelling middle-schoolers climb aboard their buses. But Ethan's dog-boy scent found me and made my insides burn. I didn't know how I would tell Mort and Drac—or worse, if I even could.

Chapter 6

After a long wait, it was apparent that Mort had forgotten about me. What was wrong with her anyway? She had a lead foot this morning, made me wear stupid, uncomfortable jeans to school, and now had the audacity to stand me up!

I stormed home, my cold blood boiling.

Once I reached our row house, I raced up the front stairs, still fuming, and flung the door open wide. It slammed into the wall with a loud thud. The handle smashed a hole in the foyer's drywall.

Mort came running into the room, cradling her favorite blue ceramic bowl in the crook of her arm. She was baking. Cookies. Hopefully chocolate chip. My mouth watered at the thought. I love sweets. Just like cafeteria food, desserts and candy don't fill me up, but unlike cafeteria food, I need them to survive. Just kidding. I wouldn't actually die without them, sometimes it just feels like that. I have a major (and slightly fanged) sweet tooth. In fact, the thought of cookies almost made me forget that I was upset. Almost.

Mort had her hair pulled back into a ponytail that swished as she moved. Little strands of baby hair fell around her face. She spied the hole in the wall, but didn't say anything, only stirred the cookie batter at a faster pace. Maybe because, for once, she was concerned about me. Maybe.

"Good thing this isn't base housing or that would come directly out of Drac's pay."

So much for caring about me. The hole seemed to grow right in front of my eyes. I cleared my throat to speak, but no words came out.

Sometimes old suckers in their vampirehood splendor had good ideas. Like deciding to buy a row house instead of living on base. My appetite for security guards wasn't good for anyone, including myself. They were loaded with hot air and made me bloated. I also rather enjoyed pets of families on the base. People were very upset when their beloved cat went missing. I couldn't help it. They begged for attention with their snobby attitudes! It wasn't my fault "attention" consisted of sucking their blood. But the best reason for living off base was because of holes in walls. It meant I wouldn't get in trouble. At least I hoped.

Mort wiped a hand on the apron tied around her waist. "Everything okay, Scarlet?"

"No." I stomped into the living room and flopped down on the couch.

"Well . . . do you want to talk about it?"

I thought for a moment. I wanted her to know I was fuming mad when she forgot to pick me up from school. I wanted to tell her about the stupid werewolf at Charles Perrault Middle school, but I figured it wasn't the best time to mention it because she would just do the parent freak-out thing, and we'd have to move. Even though I was used to moving, I hated all the packing and boxes and mess. It was just so overwhelming.

Plus if we moved, I'd miss out on getting to know a really interesting, earthy-smelling girl. A girl I had no desire of sinking my teeth into. I couldn't tell Mort anything just yet.

"Well," Mort said interrupting my thoughts. "Is there something you want to tell me?"

"It's nothing."

"Nothing, huh?"

"Just a long day, that's all."

Mort had a look on her face that told me she didn't take the bait.

I had to tell her something. "I made a friend." Technically she wasn't my friend, but it was the closest I was ever going to get. I'd never come any closer than that to fitting in with my peers. Trying to act casual, like I was a pro at the friend-making thing, I leaned back, propping my feet up on the coffee table and folded my arms behind my head. "Her name is Cindy."

"Does she know?" Mort licked her lips and gestured to

her mouth, tapping a tooth with her index finger. You'd think, after all these years, she'd come up with something a little more discreet, but no, it was the same lick-point-and-tap.

I tried really hard not to roll my eyes. "No, no. Of course not. She doesn't know a thing." I walked past her toward the fridge. "And want to know something else?"

"Hmmm?"

"No one tried to stuff me in a locker!" For added measure, I said, "And I obeyed all the rules." That's progress.

Mort followed me into the kitchen, vigorously stirring the mix in her bowl. "Good." She sighed in relief. "And try to keep it that way."

"You know I will." This was our typical, post-first-day conversation. At least that was the same when everything else was weird. I pulled open the fridge door. Cool air spilled onto my already cold, dead skin. A case of Bloody Toms sat on the top shelf.

I grabbed a can and popped it open. With my teeth. My fangs are so sharp, I don't need a can opener. Sipping slowly, I thought about Cindy. She was weird. Probably the weirdest non-dead person I'd ever met. I chugged down the rest of my drink. "You know, that Cindy girl . . . she's pretty . . ." I tossed my can in the recycling. "What's the word? Cold?"

"I think the word you're looking for is cool, honey."

"Oh, right. Cooool. Well she's cool."

Mort stopped a moment, thinking. "Though I overheard some moms at the base today. They claimed that epic was the recent word choice. One of them even mentioned a beast.

Can you imagine that? A beast is cool? I think I've heard just about everything!"

"Epic, huh? Well, then she's epic."

"Well, I'm really impressed, Scarlet." Mort cheered. "I never thought you'd make friends so soon. Those new clothes must really be doing the trick! Aren't you glad you listened to me?"

My stomach sank. Mort didn't think I could make friends by being myself? If only Mort knew just how little I fit in. One friend does not make me socially accepted by my peers. Not to mention, there was that whole wolf-boy thing. "Yeah and you know what else?"

"No, what?" Mort turned away and scooped a spoonful of dough onto a tray.

"I have no desire to suck her blood."

Mort froze in place, her shoulders going rigid and the spoon clattering to the floor. "Really?" she whispered, her voice wavering.

Mort's reaction should have been my first clue to stop talking, but sometimes I get diarrhea of the mouth and can't stop. "Yeah, it's the strangest thing. And she has this smell . . . like autumn leaves and dirt . . ."

"Autumn leaves you say . . ." Mort's gaze drifted off into space, like she was engaged deep in a memory.

I almost added that Cindy's smell reminded me of cemeteries and other scary things, but figured it was best to leave that out, since I wasn't afraid of her at all. Plus, by the looks of it, I'd probably dumped too much on Mort already.

"Yeah. But don't worry, she's super nice." I tossed my fedora onto the counter and brushed a strand of hair out of my eyes.

"What was this girl's name again?"

"Cindy. Her name is Cindy."

Mort seemed to be okay with the conversation. At least she wasn't acting strange like she had when she drove me to school. Which made me think it was a good time to mention it. "So . . . you kinda left in a hurry this morning." I reached in the fridge for a second Bloody Tom. "I mean, was everything okay? There's no problem with Drac's job or . . ."

Mort snapped out of her daze, and grabbed the spoon from the floor, placing it in the sink. She took a clean one from the drawer and stabbed it into the cookie dough. Without saying a word she turned to me and ripped the can of vegetable juice from my hand.

"I'm sorry . . . I was just . . ." I didn't realize that question would upset her so much. I guess she wasn't over the fact that they had to move again. Because of me. And my constant mess-ups. Why couldn't I ever just follow the rules? Then everyone would be happy and I wouldn't have to worry about being sent to the Underworld.

She placed the can back in the fridge, slamming the door. "You'll spoil your appetite."

"Not ferret again, is it?" I gulped, hoping she wouldn't be angry.

Mort shot me a look. But then, as if someone had flipped

a switch, she calmed. "Of course not." Mort licked her lips. "Drac's bringing home a black lab."

I held back a gag.

Did I mention I hate dogs?

Well, I do.

VAMPIRE RULE #42

Dogs are gross. Okay, so that one's not an official rule. But still, they're gross.

I prefer cats most of the time—even with their annoying, uppity attitude and all their begging for attention by snaking between your legs and meowing. "Do I have to eat it? They taste like all the nasty stuff they eat. Heck, they lap up their own vomit. And lick their butts."

Mort glared, the pale skin of her face turning a purplish-red.

"C'mon! Admit it. You know they smell! It's like a moldy dishrag that's never been washed. Or . . . or . . . or sweaty gym clothes festering in the heat of the garage." I covered my mouth. "I threw up a little just thinking about it."

My argument didn't faze Mort. So for added measure, I placed my arm to my forehead, swooning melodramatically. "Who wants to smell that when they eat?"

I braced myself for Mort to remind me about the rules.

VAMPIRE RULE #43

This one is best handled by quoting my mother: "Dogs

are not gross. You just haven't discovered their delightful, piquant flavor quite yet. With time and maturity you'll come to love them."

But instead she just gave her disapproving, don't-be-so-ungrateful-Mort look. "This one's a stray. Drac saw it on the way to work. We're doing it a favor. It would only end up at the pound."

"But . . ."

A key jingled in the lock.

Mort licked her lips. "Well, speak of the Devil himself!"

Drac burst through the back door carrying the furry, slobbery mess into the kitchen. "Dinner is served!" He stretched his lips wide, fangs jutting out.

"Smells divine," Mort whispered. "Come on Scarlet. You've got to be starving!"

Mort always became more pleasant when being fed. I think she suffers from blood sugar issues. Or something. Maybe that was it. She must have skipped breakfast.

"Eat up," Drac said. "You want to grow up big and strong, don't you?"

"No thanks." I cupped my palm over my mouth, holding back the vomit inching its way up my throat. I raced out of the kitchen. The odor was enough to gag a maggot. Or a vampire.

Plus, the worst part—the part I didn't expect at all—the smell reminded me of that Ethan boy.

Mort called after me. "I knew you'd spoil your appetite."

Chapter 7

I staggered out the front door with my backpack on my shoulder, down the steps of our row house, and onto the sidewalk.

I breathed deep, taking in the fresh air. A distant fragrance of flowers lingered in the air, reminding me of our long-ago cottage home. Sometimes I really missed living in the country. It'd been so long since I even thought about it. But you never really outgrow your first home. The one where you should have grown up to be a normal person complete with a family of your own.

I shook my head. I had to get those child-like longings out of my brain. It didn't matter that I was one hundred and thirty-six years old, because to Mort and Drac, I'd always be their little ghoul. Instead of being able to grow up, I'd always be a kid, since vampires never grow old. I was doomed to live in a perpetual state of childhood—never respected for who I was on the inside, beneath my vampire exterior. Not by my peers. And worse, not by Mort or Drac.

And kids—no matter how long they've been a kid—have dreams. Even if they are just crazy dreams. Unfortunately for me they would only remain dreams. While most parents were telling their kids to grow up, mine were telling me to act like a child. "Scarlet," Mort would say. "I know you're not twelve anymore, but you need to act like it."

How can you argue with parents who encourage childhood? I mean, that's like every kid's dream come true. Right?

And I know the old suckers loved me. They wanted the best for me no matter what.

Lately though, Mort acted weird, driving off, rushing around and hurrying me along and Drac seemed bothered by all the moving, huffing and puffing and letting bad words slip when things didn't go as planned.

Sometimes, I felt like a burden. They'd be better off without me. They could be content with their vampire ways and maybe even retire. They wouldn't have to relocate each year—or whenever I messed up—whichever comes first.

Those mistakes seemed to get closer and closer together each year.

I sucked in a long breath, but it didn't make me feel any better. So I sat down on the front steps, letting my hair fall into my face as I stared at the ground.

The door opened, and footsteps approached. "Scarlet?" Mort wiped saliva from her mouth with the back of her hand, the smell of dog lingering on her breath. She sat down, her

poodle skirt spilling onto the concrete, and wrapped her arm around my shoulder. Why was she acting all huggy-kissy-touchy-feely with me? She was doing the whole VDA thing, which was too weird of a switch from her drop-and-run this morning.

"Yeah, what?" I said, snapping at her even though I didn't really mean it. Okay. I meant it. A little.

She brushed my bangs out of my eyes. "Things will be good here." The tremble in her voice was unconvincing. I had to wonder what she held back. What she knew about things. What she kept from me. Little did she know, I kept something from her. Mort could never find out about the werewolf at Charles Perrault Middle School. If she did, we'd have to move.

Still, I couldn't seem too eager to stay here since that would be out of character, so I gave her my best middle-school attitude voice. "Let me guess." I shot her an angry glare. "You promise."

Mort didn't say anything. She just sat there. And although I could tell she was hurt, she did a good job of hiding it, forcing a feigned smile. She gave my shoulder a squeeze.

"Oh, by the way." I pulled my schedule and other paper-work from my backpack. "Here's some forms for you to sign."

Mort took the papers, her eyes fixated on the bold print at the top where it said sixth grade schedule right above my name. "Scarlet Small!" Her chest heaved as she tried to control her breathing. "Tell me you didn't disobey me. You were told to enroll in seventh grade—not sixth!"

VAMPIRE RULE #71

When it's time to move, don't complain. Be warned though—
they will force you to enroll in seventh grade instead of
sixth. This rule has some variables, including how urgent
the move is (translation: if I messed up). Better do as they
say or there will be consequences!

Mort continued to scream, saying something along the lines of: "WhyCan'tYouEverListen? YouNeverFollowDirections! DoYouRealizeWhatYou'veDoneNow? ThisMakesThingsDifficultFor AllOfUs. WhatAreWeGoingToDoWithYou? DoYouWantToHaveToLiveInTheUnderworld?"

Admittedly, it was hard to make out her words through her clenched teeth. I'm pretty sure that's what she said. There may or may not have been a few bad words thrown in there.

I nodded sheepishly. "But I was just trying—"

Mort crumpled the papers, tossed them on my lap and stormed inside.

"—to help."

The door slammed and I cringed.

Gree-aat. Good job, Scarlet. Now you've completely isolated yourself from the old suckers. Not only would I never be able to figure out why she'd acted so strange when she took me to school, but now she was mad again. I guess it didn't really matter though because Mort was the sensitive type, so even though she might be mad, she'd get over it as soon as I gave an emotional, weepy-like apology.

It was the price we'd all have to pay for having vampires living together, each of us in a state of stagnation. None of us growing older on the outside but growing ancient on the inside.

I sat on the steps a while longer, hoping the time would pass and the old suckers would go to their coffins. Mort never came back to check on me.

One by one the lights in the row houses winked out. It was about time, too, because I nearly froze my butt off. When the lights went out in my house, I thought about sneaking back in and watching stupid vampire movies undisturbed. The thought of those cheesy films (the movie industry people knew so little about us, it wasn't even funny) almost made me feel better, and a smile crept onto my face.

I was just about to head inside when a low, distant howl filled the air. As much as I hate dogs, I wished I could write off the sound as a stray mutt. But I knew better. That was a werewolf howl.

"ETHAN!" I clenched my teeth together, trying not to scream. "That freaky dog-boy is going to make my life miserable."

It didn't matter that my life already was. He would make it worse.

I might need to tell Mort and Drac about Ethan after all. Because I wouldn't be able to deal with this on my own. But I knew how the old suckers felt about moving, how they felt about my mistakes. They'd probably think I had something to do with this too. As much as I wanted to confide in them, I knew I'd never be able to. If I did, maybe they'd send me to the Underworld and save themselves the trouble.

Chapter 8

I couldn't take it anymore. Maybe it was the sudden, grating sound of the howl that pushed me over the edge, but I didn't want to think about anything anymore. Not the stupid werewolf. Not the moving. Not the constant pressure to be perfect or to fit in—which was hard enough to begin with. There's nothing like being a middle-school vampire to put a nail in your coffin! And most of all, I could not accept the way my parents didn't seem to trust me. They'd never let me grow up and be my own person. Never is a really long time because vampires live forever, you know.

So I stood up. I ran. I ran past the row houses lining my street. I ran past the stores and shops. I ran past the Parkview Cemetery with its icy, wrought-iron fence. I ran until I was on the outskirts of town.

It may have been the farthest I'd ever been from the old suckers. And for the first time in my life I might have felt a little scared. That's something I learned a long time ago and wished I'd remembered it before I took off into the night, in a strange new town.

VAMPIRE RULE # 82

Vampires might be at the top of the food chain, but that doesn't mean they can't get scared.

Ironic, right? A scared vampire.

But despite my fear, I couldn't help the thrill of excitement of my newfound independence.

To my right was a park; quiet and dark. I'm sure during the day it was filled with families; children who had parents that loved and trusted them, parents who guided their kids down the slide or helped them on the swings. But at this hour, it stretched out before me like my own private playground.

I ran through the park entrance straight to a swing. I pumped my legs, hard, until I flew through the evening air. No one watched and nothing held me back. This felt great! I was over a hundred years old. I could definitely live on my own, no problem!

Flap, flap, flap.

The swing screeched to a halt as I put my feet out, braking hard. Clouds of dust billowed into the air. What was that?

My ears were on super high alert. I needed to know what that noise was. I sniffed the air, my keen sense of smell identifying a few forest animals. No people.

Flap, flap, flap.

I drew out a small penlight I kept tucked in my pocket. You know, for emergencies. Not because I was afraid of the dark. Slowly standing up, I shined the light, illuminating my surroundings.

Something flew in the air overhead. I swung my light toward the sky.

A bat! Just above the swings. I hadn't seen one in a really long time. In fact, the last bat I'd come in contact with was just a baby. She'd gotten trapped in the attic of one of our previous homes.

I shined the light on him as he flapped around in the air. He had a beautiful brown coat and a wingspan that stretched at least a foot wide.

A Mouse-Eared bat? No, no. That wasn't it. I thought long and hard. This had to be a Pipistrelle bat because of the dark face and ears.

You'd think being a vampire would make me a bat expert, but that's a myth. I didn't know as much as I would have liked.

Way back when, there used to be lots of folk tales and legends about bats. In fact, they ran rampant through small towns. Rumors floated that bats were vampires. Or that vampires could transform into bats.

Not true.

We just like to keep them for pets. They make good company. And with their sonar skills, they can alert us of food.

That's probably how the other myth about vampires

started. The one where people think we have some sort of magical powers. Not true.

VAMPIRE RULE #19
Vampires do not have super powers.

Well, unless you count the fact that we have a really good sense of smell . . . and that we live forever. Otherwise, we're just good at taking advantage of everything around us. Like using bats to help us find food. Or using wolves to help us hunt. But we all know dogs—including wolves—are gross. And dumb.

The bat flew around, swooping and diving, his wings like fluttering leaves. As he came closer, I remembered Pipestrelle bats were mostly found in London, and we hadn't lived there for over four decades. A bell went off in my head. There was a very common bat in this region—the Big Brown bat. Or in other words, an *eptesicus fuscus.*

This was most definitely a very large, brown bat.

They like to hide in lofts and buildings—which gave me an idea! I wouldn't have to go home and face the old suckers. I could just follow him, and I'd find a place to sleep for the night.

Since big brown bats fly closer to the ground than most other bats, I had a greater chance of catching him. That way I could convince him with my super powers that he should help me.

Just kidding. I don't have super powers. We just went over this. How quickly you forget.

But if I could catch him, he'd make a great pet. And I'd really missed having a pet ever since . . .

VAMPIRE RULE # 41
Never ever mistake your pet for a meal. The guilt lingers far longer than the aftertaste.

"C'mere batty, batty, batty," I called with hands cupped around my mouth.

He landed on the top bar of the swings as if he understood.

"Can you help me?" I asked.

The bat ignored me completely. Stupid me. What was I thinking? He couldn't understand. And bats certainly couldn't talk. How could I be so silly?

The bat swooped down, caught a moth and landed back on the bar.

"Well, if you're not going to help me, at least you could leave me alone." I folded my arms in a huff.

The bat flew in front of my face. "Didn't you hear what I said?" I shooed him away. "Sheesh. You sure are an irritating bat." So much for my admiration. They might have great echo location skills, but he just became number one on the annoying scale.

FLAP.

The bat slammed into a tree and fell to the ground.

Almost like he was offended at what I'd said. "Did you really hear me? I mean, did you understand what I said?"

He lifted his little brown bat head, his black beady eyes studying me.

"Are you okay? You're not hurt are you?" I put out my hand. Normally, before my undead days, I would never touch a bat. I used to think they were scary and creepy and carried disease. But vampires are immune to diseases, including rabies. While I might avoid werewolves and dogs, it's not because of disease. It's because they stink.

The bat crawled onto my hand and inched his way up my arm onto my shoulder, snuggling into my neck.

"No biting," I said with a chuckle. "Only vampires are allowed to bite." I chomped my teeth together.

I swore the bat laughed along because he made a little squeaking sound. His head bopped up and down like Mort's shoulders when she tries to hold back a fit of the giggles.

"I need to find somewhere to sleep tonight. Can you help?"

The bat squirmed on my shoulder. He flapped his wings then flew off into the darkness.

"Well, I guess that's a no." I slumped to the ground, defeated and friendless. But a moment later the bat returned.

"Go away," I mumbled, frustrated with his flighty attitude. "I'm dead tired." If he wasn't going to be my friend, or my pet, the least he could do was let me sleep.

He dive bombed into my hair. I let out a shriek. While I

like bats, but the last place I want one is in my hair. If you've never had a bat fly into your hair, then you're in for a real treat. They get caught and it's nothing but fur, wings, and tangled tresses. Only garden sheers can take care of that kind of mess.

I flailed, swinging my arms and batting at my hair. There had to be a way to free myself from the dive-bombing, hair-attacking freak. After a struggle, my hair finally ripped from its grasp and the bat flew onto the branch of a nearby tree.

"What the heck is the matter with you?" Stupid bat. I gave him an evil-eye, which was real easy seeing as I was annoyed. Plus I'm a vampire. We're good at the evil thing. I stomped off into the darkness.

Flap, flap, flap.

I was about to turn around and scream at him when a howl filled the air. It made me feel vulnerable and scared.

"Wolf!" I whispered under my breath. That's when I remembered something awful. Something so terrible and horrible it made me quake in my shoes. Werewolves were our mortal enemies for a reason. And it wasn't just because they stink. No, it's because one bite from them will kill a vampire. I was pretty sure if Ethan found me in the park, I'd be an undead goner.

Chapter 9

My pulse thumping wildly like a terrible drum solo, I ran home. While I wanted my independence, wanted to feel accepted and loved, safety was my number one priority. Being out in the park with a lunatic werewolf on the loose wasn't exactly safe for a vampire. My feet pounded on the pavement, my breath catching in my throat like a fire. Home seemed farther than I remembered. Regret crept into my chest. Why had I been thrilled to be so far away before? All I wanted was to see my home, be inside, curled up in my coffin safe and sound.

Flap, flap, flap.

Are you kidding me? The bat was still at my side. "You're not . . . really . . . following me . . . are you?" I panted, in total disbelief that he was stalking me, especially at a time like this. I didn't need an annoying bat pestering me when my life was at stake.

The bat landed on my shoulder. I was too worried about the howling wolf to chase him off, so I let him stay there.

"Oh, now you're . . . my friend?" I said between breaths. Maybe it wasn't so bad to have him with me. Perhaps he could dive-bomb the wolf if he tried to get near me.

Wolf. The wolf!

With all the distraction from the bat and the sound of my feet as I ran, I hadn't realized that he'd stopped howling. I stopped running and lifted my nose in the air, taking a deep sniff. No disgusting doggy smell. The wolf was gone. I was sure of it. Still, I wasn't about to stay outside. I had to get home before the wolf decided to hunt me down. There was no reason to panic. At least not for a little bit.

I patted the bat on the head, feeling relieved.

"So, we're friends now?" My parents probably wouldn't like that I'd made a bat for a friend. Or that he would be my new pet. Which probably meant they'd have another reason to be angry. "Well, if that's the case, then I'll need to give you a name." I thought for a moment, wanting something perfect. "How about Shade?"

He seemed to nod in agreement.

"Shade it is!"

Happy with my new friend, I skipped along. Maybe things wouldn't be so bad here. With a pet bat, Cindy as a friend (and that Sarah girl, too), I felt sure this would be the best place yet. I'd deal with the wolf if I had to. Maybe find a way around it somehow. Throw him a bone and distract him.

With each step I began to realize the walk home seemed

to take forever. My skin crawled as I realized I'd gone too far. Or maybe even worse—I was lost. How does a vampire get lost, you ask? I don't know. I'm not the vampire rule book goddess. Actually, I kinda am. But don't ask about being lost. It just happens, okay?

I turned on my little penlight, but the battery was dead. Angry, I threw it on the ground.

VAMPIRE RULE #83

Carry a flashlight. Preferably one with working batteries. You never know when you'll get lost and might need it.

I trudged along, and no matter how many steps I took, it seemed like I'd never find my way back home. My feet were cold and wet from the dew on the grass. In fact, my toes felt like they had frostbite. Which made me really thirsty. Life sucked. But not in a good, vampire kind of way.

Just as I was about to give up, my chest aching with a sob that threatened to burst its way out, a glow from a lamppost lit my path. Two streets over was mine. What a relief!

I practically ran to my house. As I closed the door behind me, the wolf howled in the distance.

After bolting the lock, I collapsed against the door, thankful to be home. I'd find a way to deal with Mort and Drac and the threat of the Underworld and Mr. Death. I wouldn't make any more mistakes. I'd be good. Perfect.

Shade rubbed his head against my neck and my undead heart skipped a beat. If Mort and Drac found Shade, I'd be in trouble. Just in case the old suckers woke up, I hid him beneath layers of my long hair and crept up to my room.

"Good night, Shade," I whispered as he flew up to the rafters and hung upside down. He blended in perfectly with the dark wood. No one would ever see him there. My coffin beckoned to me and I curled up, snug as a bug in a rug. Sleep came quickly. Dreams of my new friends brought a feeling of peace. Something I hadn't had in a long time.

It seemed like only moments had passed when Mort opened the lid to my casket and shook my shoulder. "You'll be late for school." The tone in her voice told me she was in a killer mood. Usually she'd sing this silly little song about 'neck'tarines and blood oranges and my mouth would get all drooly.

Light seeped into my casket and I sat up quickly. Suddenly dizzy, I rubbed my palms against my eyes. "What time is it?" I mumbled, still half-asleep.

"Seven," Mort said taking a deep sniff of air before marching out of the room.

"Seven already?" I felt so confused. It seemed I'd only just gotten home from my adventure in the park . . . with a bat . . . Shade! I scanned my room. Where was he? Was it all just a dream? I leapt out of my coffin, threw on my robe, and followed Mort down the stairs. Shade wasn't anywhere to be found. He wasn't hanging from any of the cupboards in the kitchen.

Mort went straight to the fridge and pulled out a can

of vegetable juice and tossed it to me. "Drink fast, then get dressed."

I spaced out as I tossed the can between my hands.

"What's wrong?" Mort asked defensively.

My gaze drifted to her and she scowled. For the first time I noticed her bloodshot eyes. It made me kind of hungry. "Nothing," I said, wondering why Mort looked so terrible. Maybe she hadn't been sleeping well.

"You want something more gourmet? Cougar perhaps?" Mort sniffed the air again.

Did she smell Shade? Or could she smell the fresh air on my clothes from being gone all night? "Huh?"

"Gourmet breakfast," Mort snapped. "Get it yourself." She motioned to the back door. "There's a forest, right there. You'll find plenty to hunt there."

I hadn't been to the forest and the idea made me perk up. "Oh." I looked at the can of vegetable juice in my hands. "No. This'll be just fine." I slid my nail under the tab and popped the lid open, which was unusual for me. Normally I just sunk my sharp fangs into it. For some reason I felt dazed.

The can felt cold against my lips. The metal tasted stronger than usual, so I only took a little sip. Usually I liked the metallic taste; it reminded me of good, strong, iron-rich blood.

Mort tapped her watch, taking another whiff of air. "If you don't hurry, you'll have to walk to school."

I wouldn't—couldn't—let her threats bother me. "Fine."

I shrugged, feeling defeated by her new attitude, which seemed a little crazy. Maybe Mort wasn't a morning person anymore. There had to be a reason why she was so cranky lately.

"Fine." Mort glared, her hard, angry eyes a stark contrast against her soft, pale face. She grabbed her keys and headed out the front door, her flowery dress swishing with each step. She was definitely more peeved than I thought she would be. All this because I skipped dinner? Okay, and maybe I acted sarcastic and rude, but still. Maybe she's still mad that I enrolled in sixth grade. Either way, she seemed to be overreacting.

Oh no! Maybe she knew I'd run off after dark. But if she knew about that, then I'd for sure be in big trouble. It would be the last straw before she sent me to the Underworld.

But I noticed that she paused—for a brief second—stealing a quick glance in my direction, before closing the door behind her.

If I didn't know better, I might have thought she felt bad. Or disappointed.

I gaped at the door, wondering if maybe I should run after her. If I called her name, she'd open her arms and hug me. Just like in the movies. Then everything would be okay and life here would be perfect. I'd have a pet. And friends. And parents who loved and accepted me. We'd all have that little bit of vampire heaven we've searched for all these years.

My feet moved before my brain could catch up. But as I approached the door, my hand touching the cool brass handle, I heard the engine hiss and pop. I peered out the window. Mort's car chugged down the road, the engine sputtering the whole way.

I sighed. Too late. I climbed the stairs to my room.

"Shade?" I glanced around. "C'mere batty, batty, batty." Great. My bat was gone, too, which made me feel horrible.

Whatever. That dingbat probably never thought we were friends. He'd only be a nuisance anyway, just like all my other pets were.

VAMPIRE RULE # 40

Don't think that just because your pet is an animal—and animals are hunters—that they're okay with the whole vampire thing. Seriously, animals are not stupid. Pets know predators when they see one. Especially labrador retrievers. They're smarter than they look.

Frustrated, I got dressed into the uncomfortable clothes Mort had bought and grabbed my bag. There was still no sign of the bat. Figures. Friends never stick around when you're a middle-school vampire. Not like I needed him anyway.

I stepped out into the cool morning and started on my way to school. Halfway there, I heard a voice.

Chapter 10

My super-vampire powers sensed it was Cindy. Just kidding. I knew it was her because of the earthy-smell that crept into my nose.

"Hey, Cindy." Without ever looking at her, I slowed my pace so she could catch up.

Her feet pitter-pattered on the pavement until she was at my side. "You late, too?" She looked at me strangely.

Maybe she was shocked I knew it was her before I even saw her. Which reminded me to try to blend in, act normal. "I overslept. You?"

"Yeah, me too." She shoved a paper in her pocket. "Night owl?"

"Huh?" Humans said the weirdest things sometimes.

Cindy laughed. "Do you like to stay up late?"

"Oh." So that's what a night owl was—someone who liked to stay up late. I wondered what they called vampires who were night owls. Nothing, probably. We were all night owls. We couldn't escape the bitemares. "Yeah, yeah. Up all night."

"Did you just fall asleep," Cindy laughed mid-sentence, "only to wake at the butt-crack of dawn?"

Snort! This girl was too funny. "Yeah, it felt like it this morning," I said, a smile spreading across my face. I couldn't believe I was giggling and . . . fitting in!

"I totally slept through the sun coming up."

"Oh," Cindy said with surprise. "I m-mean, me t-too," she stuttered.

What was it with everyone lately? They all seemed to be hiding something. Mort with her attitude and air sniffing. And Ethan. Technically he didn't hide anything. It was obvious he was a stupid wolf-boy. What more was there to know about a werewolf other than they smell nasty? And that if he bit me I'd die a painful, undead death. Now Cindy seemed to have secrets too.

I shook my head. Nah. She was way too normal.

She linked her arm with mine, the fragrance of autumn leaves and earth filling the air around us, and we stepped in rhythm. Before long, our steady march merged into a full-fledged skip.

Remembering when I was younger and I had real-live friends, I did the only thing I knew. I sang at the top of my lungs. Feeling at ease, I couldn't hold it back and I sang at the top of my lungs. "Skip to my lou . . . lou . . . skip to my LOOOUUU!"

Cindy turned to look at me, her eyebrows wrinkling together.

"What?" My smile dropped I hid behind my bangs. Guess she thought that song was for babies. Plus, it was probably as ancient as me.

Cindy's elbow yanked mine. "Swing your partner round and round . . ." Cindy sang as she changed direction, dancing and skipping as she pulled me in a square dance fashion.

For the first time in a very long time, I felt like a silly schoolgirl. Maybe at my age (I mean my real age that I should be had I never become a vampire), I shouldn't have enjoyed it so much. But it was hard to be so old and yet so young at the same time. I know people who would give up just about anything to be young again. Who was I to complain about it?

In science, Mrs. Femur mentioned we needed to do a review. So she lectured us about bones and the skeletal system. Cindy raised her hand and answered all the questions. Mrs. Femur patted her on the head with each correct response.

VAMPIRE RULE #50
Don't answer too many questions, especially during your first week. It draws attention. Then teachers expect you to be their pet. And pets are dumb.

I was just glad we weren't discussing blood disorders and diseases. It would make me super thirsty. That wouldn't be good for anyone in the room.

Later, in history class, Mrs. Frankensheimer passed out notes about World War II.

My eyes scanned the page, and I noticed the error right away. I've lived just about every part of modern history, so I know it all too well. Textbooks always get stuff wrong. Plus, some people seem to like re-writing history. Unless you've got a time machine, facts are facts and you can't change them. "Ummm . . . excuse me." My hand shot into the air like a missile. "Mrs. Frankensheimer, I think there's a mistake on this paper."

"Oh, really? What do you think is wrong, Miss . . . Miss . . ." Mrs. Frankensheimer slid her bottle-cap glasses to the tip of her pointy nose and narrowed her yes. "What was your name again?"

"Scarlet," I said, sitting tall and proud. "Scarlet Small."

"Well—Scarlet Small—do tell me where you think my error is." Mrs. Frankensheimer crossed her arms, her frizzy skunk-striped hair standing upright with static-electricity.

She rubbed me the wrong way. My lips started parting, teeth growing. Uh. Oh. Remember the rules, Scarlet!

There were two rules that I hadn't been so good at keeping in the past.

VAMPIRE RULE #55

Don't bite teachers. Even though they're not quite human—and technically you can get away with it because of rules #1 and #2—it should be avoided. It just doesn't look good on the report card. Plus you'll only get detention. And detention is super boring.

VAMPIRE RULE #60

Don't bite teachers. Even when they act stupid by misquoting Edgar Allen Poe and Jane Austen. Or try to re-write history because they think they know so much about Hitler.

I thought about the old suckers and my promise to be good, fit in. Even if Mort had been acting cranky, I couldn't give us away. There was no telling what would happen if people found out there were vampires living in their town. "Never mind. My mistake." I sank into my chair.

Mrs. Frankensheimer pushed her glasses back into position, her eyes looking huge behind the thick, bottle-cap lenses. "That's what I thought." She turned her back and bustled to the board, her pointy heels clicking with each step. "Now, open your books . . ."

Cindy leaned closer, pressing a note into my palm. I unfolded it in my lap. It said:

Watch out for that one! She can be nasty. But I've got your back. Circle yes or no if you've got mine, too.

I nodded and mouthed 'thank you.' This girl really watched out for me! Isn't that what friends do? I couldn't be sure. It had been so long since I'd had a friend, a real friend—someone I could trust—that it felt impossible to know the difference.

As soon as class ended, Cindy grabbed my hand and pulled me to her locker. "You've got to watch out for that one," she reminded

"I see that," I grumbled. "Thanks. For, you know . . ." I rubbed my arm awkwardly. ". . . the warning." This friend thing felt strange.

"Anytime," Cindy said as she shuffled through her things.

Sarah sulked up to her locker. She whispered something into Cindy's ear. They seemed to have a conversation with their eyes, even though I could only see part of their faces. Cindy shut the metal door with a clang. "Gotta run." She placed her hand on my shoulder. "But I'll see you at lunch."

"Right." I nodded as she wrapped an arm around Sarah and headed off without me. Maybe I was wrong about this friendship thing.

Chapter 11

By the time I reached the cafeteria, Cindy and Sarah had disappeared in the crowd. Why neither of them waited for me was a mystery.

So far, this was not shaping up to be a great second day. What with no sleep, a near-tardy to school, narrowly escaping a chewed-up-and-spit-out episode by Mrs. Frankensheimer, and my almost-friend ditching me right before lunch, it made me feel all trembly.

Stress usually takes away my appetite, which is a good thing for neighborhood animals and an even better thing for yummy smelling middle-schoolers.

Yet, I found that this stress was different. I was starving! I could eat a horse. For real. You know how many quarts of blood are in a horse? Me either. But I bet it's a lot!

I glanced at the kids waiting in line, glad I'd thought to bring a sack lunch today. Cafeteria food is the closest thing to MRE's ("Meals Ready to Eat"—that's military food the troops have to eat, but Drac says they should really be called "Meals Refused by Ethiopians" because even starving people in Ethiopia won't eat them, they taste so bad). Once I left an entire school lunch on my dresser to see how long it would take before it grew mold. But it never got moldy. Heck, it never even decomposed! That stuff was a single molecule away from being plastic. I glared at the substance they called food, displayed behind glass in giant silver serving dishes. A warming light glowed above, making the meal appear even more foreign.

The menu: a rectangular shaped piece of cardboard, smothered in red sauce. A grated plastic substance passed off as cheese, though I'm sure it tasted like rubber. The lunch ladies usually referred to this garbage as pizza.

There was salad. Don't kid yourself into thinking it was fresh, with crispy leaves and tasty shredded carrots. Nope. This was nothing more than slimy, green mush.

At the end of the counter, fruit cups were displayed on flesh colored trays. Those fruit cups consisted of three chunks of unidentifiable orange-colored squares sustained in a sugar-laden jelled substance geared to disguise its true taste.

Yup. It was a typical middle school cafeteria lunch.

Disgusted, I took my bag and sat at a table in a dark corner of the cafeteria. Normally, it would be the reject table, but I chased away anyone who tried to sit there. They didn't exactly like the look I gave them. I may or may not have showed my fangs.

VAMPIRE RULE #16

Always use good manners. Translation: Don't show your fangs in public.

I plucked my sand-witch out of my brown paper bag. Yes, sand-witch. They're a delicacy. Witches are nasty folk, so I don't feel bad slapping them between a couple slices of bread. Besides, if I couldn't have vampire food, I had to eat something. If I didn't munch away during lunch like all the other kids, I'd stand out like a sore thumb.

My chewing slowed as the tell-tale dog smell seeped in and ruined the taste of my sand-witch.

Ethan! I thought, grinding my teeth together.

Would he be dumb enough to reveal his wolfie-self to the entire school? Glancing out from behind my bangs, I watched him. His smooth stride, his perfect clothes, and neatly kept hair. Nah. Even though he was a stupid dog-boy, it was obvious he cared too much about appearances. Plus he was in human form. Ethan was only dangerous when he was a full-fledged werewolf.

I glanced down at my favorite pair of boots, my skinny jeans, which still felt uncomfortably tight, and my name-brand shirt Mort had picked out. I cared about the way I was dressed because for the second day in a row, I felt like a freak, even if I did look exactly like all my classmates. Except for my hair. Other than my razor sharp fangs, it was my best quality.

Dog-boy plopped his tray on the table, making me jump. He sat, facing me, a smirk on his face revealing his big, white teeth. He ran his fingers through his matted fur, I mean wavy hair, before he picked up his fork and stabbed it into his fruit cup. He shoved the bite in his mouth and chomped down. As I sat there in disgust, watching wolf-boy devour his food just like a real dog, I wondered where Cindy was. She promised she'd see me at lunch. Where was she? And where was Sarah?

Hunter sat next to him, without saying a word. He acknowledged me with a head-nod, and then nudged his brother. They exchanged a glance, then looked at me together.

Ethan slammed his fork down onto his tray, and I jumped at the sudden gesture. The silver of the fork glistened like a mirror, his reflection revealed within the prongs. I peered at it, suddenly realizing . . .

Oh no! I couldn't let him see that I didn't have a reflection. If he did, he'd know I was a vampire! There's no telling what a werewolf would do with a secret like that.

I had to think fast. What could I do? My stomach lurched with fear and I grabbed my napkin to cover my mouth. That's it! Before he could notice my non-reflection, I threw my napkin onto his fork.

Ethan's jaw propped open, revealing his chewed-up food.

"Gross!" I squealed. "There was a bug. In your lettuce." It was the only thing I knew to do to protect myself and my family's secret.

Ethan seemed to grow agitated, his face burning red. Hunter quickly bowed his head and his shoulders shook. Was he holding back a laugh? Were they laughing at me? Making fun of me?

"A green one. Covered in fur." My voice dripped with sarcasm. "Kind of like you." I was egging him on, even if I shouldn't.

A deep rumble, something like a growl, came from Ethan. Hunter leaned over and whispered something to him I couldn't hear.

Oops! What was I thinking? I'd definitely gone too far. Now dog-boy would find me after school, probably when it was dark. He'd infect me with his poison and I'd be a dead man. But what could I do now? Nervous, I took a bite of my sand-witch, chewing slowly, waiting for his next move.

Ethan scowled, grabbed his fork and lifted it into the air. The silver sparkled in the light. With a grand flourish, he rotated the fork between his fingers, like a color guard twirling a wand. He threw the fork into the air, letting it twist acrobatically a few times, before catching it in his palm.

As I watched his performance, my eyes felt as if they twinkled like a star-struck groupie meeting the famous heart-throb for the first time. Except Ethan was not a heart-throb. He was a gross wolf-boy. Was there something I didn't know? Did wolves have super powers? Could he charm me with his magic?

Our eyes locked.

Ethan wrapped his hand tight around the handle, smirking.

Oh-my-vampire-heck! What was wrong with this freak?

Ethan inched closer, the fork still gripped between his fingers.

Then he stabbed me!

Chapter 12

H E STABBED MY HAND WITH A FORK!

VAMPIRE RULE #120

Refer to vampire rule #21—Vampires feel pain. Good under-taker almighty, they feel pain.

VAMPIRE RULE #121

Especially on special occasions, like when a werewolf drives a metal fork into their hand.

A spark of anger lit within me, growing hotter and hotter until rage burned in my gut. It flamed like the fires from deep within the Underworld. I should know—every vampire goes there, right as they transition from human to vamp. It's not exactly a nice place. Mr. Death, the Undertaker, yeah . . . he's kind of a creeper.

Pain shot through my hand and I let out a yelp. Even though I wanted to cry, I didn't. Ethan didn't deserve the satisfaction my tears would bring. His hand shot out, grabbing for mine, but I jerked away, pulling the fork out of my skin. "What's wrong with you?" I rubbed my hand but it still tingled and ached.

Ethan gaped at me, the disbelief on his face making my insides flop. "I didn't . . ." He turned toward Hunter. "You . . ." But Hunter grabbed his tray and high-tailed it out of the cafeteria.

The fire raged. That dog-boy would pay! Police would be calling his family and loved ones to gather around his dearly departed body. He was the bane of my existence and I would make sure he knew it—for all eternity!

Or the rest of his days at Charles Perrault Middle School. Whichever came first.

I stalked around the table until I was face to face with the wolf-boy, his hot, smelly breath searing off my nose hairs. I balled my good hand into a fist. My nails bit into my palm, sending a sharp pain shooting up my arm. With all the force I could muster, I reared back and punched Ethan square on his nose. He flew back. A stream of blood winged through the air, straight at me and splattered on my face. Normally I adore the sweet fragrance of blood, being a vampire and all, but this was Ethan we're talking about. It was gross.

Even so, as I wiped it off, I smiled smugly, crossing my

arms with a satisfied sigh. Ethan got what he deserved. Stupid dog-faced boy.

Except . . . I noticed how a hush fell over all the other middle-schoolers in the cafeteria.

They were all staring.

Which meant I'd drawn attention to myself. Not smart. Why couldn't I ever just fit in? Why couldn't I control my emotions? Or follow the rules. If Mort and Drac found out what I'd done, I'd be in an Underworld of hurt. My throat squeezed tight as I fought back tears. Not only because I knew I'd face punishment, but because I felt sorry for punching Ethan . . . even if he did stab my hand with a fork.

Eyes of every sixth grader at Charles Perrault Middle School stared at me, judging and disapproving. I'm sure they were perfect. Not. "What are you staring at?" I growled.

One by one the kids resumed eating, chatting and laughing. After a few minutes, most of them acted like nothing ever happened.

I sulked back to my seat. When I sat down, I peered up through my dark bangs.

Cindy stood there, at the end of the table, with her arms folded across her chest. Her gaze shot back and forth between me and Ethan, like she was piecing the puzzle together in her head. The fork marks in my hand. The splattered blood. Ethan's dripping nose.

Tears flooded Cindy's eyes as she took in the scene.

Oh no! What had I done? Poor Cindy. She would hate me now!

Poor me. I just ruined any shot I had of ever fitting in. Of ever having a chance at a real friend.

Good going, Scarlet. My undead heart sank to my toes.

"What's wrong with you?" Cindy said, as she stalked over to Ethan who lay in a heap against the far wall in the cafeteria.

It was a good question. Unfortunately, I didn't have an answer for her because I didn't really know what was wrong with me either. Except I felt threatened and scared by a were-wolf, I'd never fit in and I was terribly misunderstood.

"How could you do something so mean?" Cindy's voice quivered. "And awful. And . . ."

Well, that about summed it up. I was mean. I was awful. And I always would be. I'd never be good. I was a vampire.

VAMPIRE RULE #123

Don't make friends. Ever. Because you'll just do something stupid that confirms 'vampire' and 'good' can never exist in the same sentence. Neither can 'vampire' and 'friend' for that matter.

My eyes pleaded with Cindy. A small part of me, buried deep in my gut beneath a century of vampire torment, wished I was capable of being something else. Anything else.

But Cindy wasn't sympathetic. Her glare shot straight to my core—right where my undead heart should beat. Shame flooded my body like a big, dark, ugly monster. I'd risked my one and only friendship for the sake of getting even with a werewolf, who wasn't even worth the energy. And I was sure, more now than ever before, that as soon as Ethan was in his werewolf form, he'd come for me. He'd make sure he ripped me to shreds. Show me who was boss.

My gaze drifted from Cindy to Ethan, who lay there gritting his teeth. He practically frothed and foamed at the mouth. I couldn't blame him. Even if he did stab my hand with a fork, he didn't deserve what I'd done.

Cindy helped Ethan to his feet. Blood still dripped from his nose. "You okay?" She placed a napkin to his face, dabbing at the blood. Once he was cleaned up, Cindy leaned close to him, pressing her head to his shoulder in a hug.

Ethan nodded, slowly, carefully, methodically. His gaze didn't stray from mine. Ethan's eyes turned into glowing slits of green. He stretched his arm outward and pointed. "Watch it Scarlet," he growled.

Chapter 13

D ead meat—that was me. My life was over. Well, technically it ended a century ago when I died. But my vampire life was over, for sure. A lump formed in my throat.

VAMPIRE RULE #124
Don't make werewolves angry. Their revenge is worse than their smell. Whoever said their bark was worse than their bite was a giant, big-headed liar!

My knees knocked in fear. Trust me when I say I peed a little.

"You know, Scarlet, I'm a pretty forgiving person." Cindy's voice trembled. "But this is just . . ." She searched for words, a tear leaking from the corner of her eye. ". . . unforgiveable."

My stupid heart sank in my chest. Why was I such a

horrible person? I'd been through so much—if people could only understand that. But they'd never know. I couldn't ever tell them. Instead I'd have to just deal with looking (and acting) like a complete jerk. Forever.

"I'm sorry," I managed to squeak out. "I . . . I didn't mean it." Those words seemed to form in my mouth an awful lot lately. When would I ever learn?

"I don't know how friends treat each other where you're from, but here we start by not punching each other." Cindy wiped away her tears.

Even though I wanted to tell her that Ethan started it, I figured that would make me sound too much like a toddler tattling on a bratty sibling.

But . . . if the shoe fits.

"Ethan started it!" I blurted out. Man, I had no filter on my thoughts—or my mouth! "He stabbed his fork into my hand."

Cindy paused, lifted her gaze level with Ethan's and dropped the napkin on the floor. "Is that true?"

She probably suspected it was true though. She'd seen the fork on the table and the marks on my hand.

Ethan shrugged.

Good job Ethan. Keep it up. That shrugging thing is really working for you. Not.

"Did you stab her hand?" Cindy's brow scrunched together on her forehead. If I didn't know any better, I'd think Mort was in the room because Cindy kind of sounded like an adult.

Ethan shrugged again.

I folded my arms, tapping my foot. C'mon, wolf-boy. Try me. This was my chance to make amends. I couldn't let him mess it up for me.

Ethan hung his head. "Yes," he admitted.

Justice! I tossed my hair off my shoulders, straightening my posture. Once Cindy learned the truth, she'd be willing to forgive me. At least I hoped.

Ethan sheepishly lowered his gaze until his eyes met with Cindy's. "I'm sorry." He stuck out his lower lip in a pouty face. A wad of dog drool dripped from his mouth. So gross.

Cindy slipped her hand in his and squeezed. "It's okay."

What was up with that? "Wait a minute." I felt so betrayed. "I apologize and it's unforgiveable, but he gives you puppy dog eyes and everything is fine?"

"Shake," Cindy demanded.

I waited for Ethan to do some sort of werewolf trick, maybe a doggie roll, fur bursting out, saliva flinging across the room, but he just stared.

"Shake," Cindy commanded again.

There were things I just would never understand and a headache festered from all the drama. My forehead ached and so did my heart. I rubbed my brow, willing the pain to leave. Ethan reached out, pawing at my hand. Awh! How cute.

"Now sit!" I pointed a finger at the floor.

Cindy looked like steam would come out of her ears. She would lose it any minute and bite my head off. Personally,

I preferred the neck. "I mean shake hands and make up," she said.

Oh, right. Of course that's what she meant.

Ethan gave me his furry dog hand and I reached out to shake it but had to turn my head so the smell of dog didn't overpower my nostrils and make me keel over. I held my breath since plugging my nose would have been rude.

"Sorry . . ." I struggled to say with a lung full of air. "I shouldn't . . ."

"Me too," he said insincerely as he squeezed my hand. Hard. It felt like all the bones would shatter, but I grit my teeth, refusing to give him the satisfaction.

He loosened his grip, but continued to hold my hand in his. His hand was warm, all sweaty and gross. I pulled away sharply, but slipped and flew backward, smacking Cindy on the cheek in the process. Landing with a thud, my forehead slammed against the tile floor.

Stars flashed and floated in my vision. I sat up, noticing the mark on Cindy's face. Oh no! "You okay?" I ignored the pain radiating throughout my skull.

Cindy rubbed her cheek. "Yeah, I'm fine." She took my hand and pulled me upright. "But you . . . you're a mess."

She was right. Between the blood splatters from Ethan's nose, the fork marks in my hand and the lump forming on my head, I probably looked like I belonged in a boxing ring and not a middle school cafeteria.

Chapter 14

"You what?" Mort's voice pierced through my skull, making the knot on my head throb worse.

"Made friends," I replied sheepishly. I guess I didn't realize that was such a bad thing. I mean, I'd told her about Cindy on the first day and she seemed fine with it. Why would it suddenly become an issue?

"Not that part," Mort said, rubbing her brow. "The part about the fork, and the punching and the . . ."

"Oh right. That." I pulled my sweater tighter around me. "It was an accident."

"I don't think a boy stabbing you in the hand with a fork was an accident." Mort sighed, defeated, as she fell into a chair. "You threw something red on it, right? Ketchup, sauce from your pizza, tomato juice . . . something. Anything!"

"What . . . what for?"

"You know, Scarlet, normal people bleed when they're

stabbed with a fork. You'd think by now you'd understand how to look normal."

She's right. I never bled when Ethan stabbed me. How could I be so stupid? "No one noticed, Mort. I swear." Except maybe Hunter. He'd sure taken off in a hurry. I rubbed at the fork marks on the back of my hand.

But Mort didn't buy it. She called Drac at his office. "No take-out tonight," she said.

I knew the code. Hunting was too risky now. And it was all because of me.

"What are we going to do now?" She wrung her hands as she paced from room to room.

I shrugged.

Mort paced. I sat silently on the couch as I awaited my doom. Would this be the final straw?

Sometime later, the door flew open and Drac stormed in. He didn't say anything. He didn't have to.

I fixed my eyes on the walls as the old suckers debated our next move.

My stomach grumbled. Two nights in a row without a hunt were going to be the death of me, if my parents didn't handle that first.

"Scarlet, why don't you go to your coffin?" Mort didn't bother looking in my direction; instead, she and Drac exchanged a conversation with their eyes. I knew not to argue.

VAMPIRE RULE #130

Don't argue with the old suckers, no matter how weird they can be with their strange eye-conversations and whisper-talking. Especially when they whisper-talk.

In my room I heard Mort and Drac whispering.

"... can't handle this ..."

"... find a way ..."

"... over soon ..."

Over soon? Were they really going to get rid of me? I forced a lump in my throat into my stomach. No, they'd never do that. They couldn't. I'd be good. I'd do anything they wanted. The Underworld would be torture—they couldn't send me there.

The night faded into morning, the glow of dawn on the horizon. Before either of my parents rolled out of their coffins, I dressed and headed out the door. It would be hours before school started, but I really needed something to eat. If I didn't have a meal, my classmates were going to be in trouble. Just a small, quick hunt. Even a measly squirrel would do. I remembered that Mort had told me I could hunt in the forest behind the house. Bonus—maybe I'd see Shade again! It would be the perfect place to find a meal where I would remain unseen. Even though I was exploring somewhere new, I was sure I wouldn't get lost. So I grabbed my bag and headed toward the forest.

Past the school, I saw it. A forest, thick with trees and shrubbery. Although it was quiet, most animals still slumbering, the air smelled rich with tasty snacks. Badger, beaver, chickadee, chipmunks, fox, rabbit, raccoon and of course, squirrel. I followed the scent of rabbit. They are good, tasty game. Easy enough to hunt and still worth the effort. Their feet make for nice little good luck charms, too. Though I think that trend died a few decades ago.

I darted between trees, so silently I could be mistaken for a summer breeze. My hair trailed behind like black smoke, my bangs swooping past my eyes and flying out like little wings.

A squirrel rustled through a pile of decaying leaves. He probably thought he was safely hidden away, but I could see his little bushy tail twitching, like a not-dead-yet possum lying on the side of the road.

Just as I was about to take my chance—the opportunity golden—a loud crash scared the squirrel away. Stupid dog! Dogs can never keep quiet. Begging for approval, panting with those dopey expressions . . . At least vampires know how to be stealthy. My stomach grumbled, my mouth still wet with drool, anticipating the tasty snack I'd just missed.

A low growl burned and rumbled in my chest, until I couldn't take it anymore and I finally let it out. Loud and fierce. Things had just built up too much; Ethan-being-a-stupid-werewolf-and-ruining-everything, Cindy-whom-I-couldn't-quite-figure-out, my-parents-being-completely-unreasonable-and-never-understanding me and, this whole-vampire-who's-never-going-to-fit-in-thing. Plus I was starving!

"AAAAAHHHH!" With all the energy I could summon, I took off running, determined to find myself a meal. Off to my left, a crinkle in the leaves. I whipped my head in the direction of the sound and stood as still as possible. There's no way I would miss my meal this time.

I pounced, lightning fast, grabbing a squirrel from a pile of logs. My hands clenched tight around his torso. While squirrels weren't quite as nasty as subway rats, they didn't have quite the same fresh taste of the other forest animals. That's why we called them forest rats. It was the best way to describe them.

Mouth drooling, I inched the squirrel closer to my mouth as it squirmed in my hands.

The hairs stood up on the back of my neck. I sensed it before I heard it, freezing in place.

A werewolf stepped out from behind a tree. My breath caught in my throat, pulse pounded in my ears. Ethan! Without a doubt it was him. I'd recognize his doggy smell anywhere. And his glowing green eyes.

My hands trembled and the squirrel almost dropped from my hands. The hunger pangs kicked in and instinctively I gripped him tighter.

The wolf stalked forward, steady and slow. My knees knocked in fear. What could I do? I couldn't outrun him. There was nowhere to go. No safety for a vampire.

He could kill me with one bite. No one knew I was in the

woods. They'd never know what happened to me. Maybe it was for the best. Mort and Drac wouldn't have to deal with my anymore.

Ethan growled. He snarled his lip, exposing his big white teeth. He gnashed them together in an angry fit of rage, wads of spit flying out to the side and landing on the bark of giant oak. A tree! That was my chance for survival.

My feet pounded against the ground, leaves and moss mashing beneath my shoes. I jumped and grabbed onto a branch, the wolf's hot breath falling on my back. Scurrying up the tree just like the squirrel I kept gripped in my hand, I made it to safety.

"Try to get me up here. Sucker!"

Ethan pawed at the base of the tree and howled. He couldn't get to me if he wanted to. I laughed at my cleverness as I looked down into Ethan's glowing green eyes.

He whimpered and cried, pacing at the base of the tree.

Stupid, temperamental werewolves. My stomach growled and I looked at the squirrel again. Time for a snack. Now that I wasn't at risk of being eaten by the stupid beast of a dog, I could enjoy my meal uninterrupted.

I raised the squirrel closer to my mouth, limp in my hands. Probably playing dead. Or maybe I really had scared it to death.

But then I noticed an expression on dog-boy's face. Was he worried? Confused? Maybe he was gassy. Dogs have the stinkiest farts ever. I hoped he wouldn't let one rip while I was around.

The forest rat squirmed, coming back to life as if it knew it had moments to live. I glanced between it and Ethan, realizing something very important. If I chomped into this little guy, Ethan would know my secret. Normal people don't eat squirrels. Well, unless you're from West Virginia. But seriously, only vampires sucked blood from living things. I couldn't possibly let him know. He wasn't to be trusted. Not just because of the werewolf thing, but because he'd stabbed my hand with a fork. There was no telling what he'd do with my secret.

Chapter 15

My mouth watered, wishing I could fill my belly with a much needed meal. But protecting myself and my family remained more important. So I kissed the forest rat on the top of his head.

"Hey, wittle guy, aren't you a wittle cu-tee," I said in my best toddler-like voice as I patted his head. His soft, warm fur reminded me of Mort's favorite coat. "I wish I could bwing you home and keep you as a pet forewer and ewer."

Cold drops of sweat formed on my lip. What if I wasn't able to trick Ethan? Would wolf-boy try to make a meal out of me? Or would he just poison me with one bite? I didn't know which was worse. "But Mom doesn't wike wittle pets."

Ethan panted, with a dopey-eyed expression, his head tilting with each word I muttered.

He bought it! Phew!

"So I'm gonna wet you go now." I stroked the forest rat

one last time. I held my hand out and opened my palm. The squirrel leapt into the air, landing on a nearby branch. But then he changed directions and scampered back to my still outstretched hand. He placed one tiny foot on my finger and bit me!

"Ouch!" I yelped. "Bad forest rat!"

He dashed off, chitter-chattering. But I swear he really laughed.

Once the rat scampered up the tree and out of sight, Ethan licked his chops. He put his muzzle in the air and howled.

I didn't need to wait for him to finish to fall victim to whatever his next move might be, because he took off running, deep into the forest. As soon as he fled out of sight, I took off like a bat out of . . . well . . . you know where. Which made me think of Shade, the bat I'd befriended. Where was he anyway? I wondered if I'd ever see him again.

I ran until I reached the middle school. Lucky for me, kids overflowed onto the sidewalk from their buses. Just in case Ethan returned, I'd be able to blend in with the crowd. Well, as much as I could anyway. Some of my classmates had already reached the front doors. I lumbered past them, straight to my locker and scrambled the combination. After grabbing a few of my books, I hurried to homeroom.

The morning announcements boomed over the loud-speakers.

"Beeeee sure to join us tomorrow afternoon from noon until four at the Busy Bee School Carnival. We'll have games,

prizzzzes and our traditional pie-eating contest. Volunteering earns double community service hours. You'll have a honey of a time." Ms. Lily's voice sounded more cheerful than normal this morning. She must have gotten a good night's sleep for once in her life. Still, her emphasis on the bee puns made me nauseated.

Cindy leaned across the desk. "So you going?"

I shrugged. A carnival was the last thing on my mind. The run-in with wolf-boy left me out of sorts. Other things seemed more important. Grabbing a meal being one of them.

"You should. I hear its lots of fun."

I shrugged again, not knowing what to say. It's not like I could tell her what I'd just gone through. The carnival seemed trivial.

"Besides, I hear Principal Petto can really pack away the pies." Cindy snickered but I just rolled my eyes. "Oh, c'mon. We can go together."

"Fine," I said, crossing my arms. "But I'm not going to have any fun." I'd been to a million of those silly school things, but it was the first time I'd be going with a friend.

Cindy pretended to pout, sticking out her bottom lip. "Of course not. No fun." She crossed her finger over her heart. "Promise."

The morning passed in a blur as I hurried to my classes.

Thankfully, I managed to avoid seeing Ethan until lunch, but even then I wasn't afraid of him. Not here when he looked like a normal human boy, since I knew it was the wolf in him I really needed to fear. The smell of his dogginess took away my appetite. Which was a good thing since I never got to have that snack this morning and middle-schoolers were looking more and more tempting each and every second.

Ethan took a sizeable bite from a ketchup-loaded hamburger. Glops of the red paste dropped from the bun, landing on the tray in front of him. It dribbled down his shirt and smeared around the corners of his mouth.

It reminded me of my first vampire kill, the messy tastiness of it. Drool cascaded down my lips in a waterfall. The acids in my stomach bubbled, the ache of hunger burning like a fire.

Normally ketchup is so gross, but right then it just reminded me of blood. And I was hungry.

Too hungry.

Ethan made disgusting chewing and slobbering noises with each bite. "What's the matter Scarlet? Hungry?"

The way he said that word really irked me. It was obvious. He deliberately tempted me.

I clenched my fists, realizing I'd been leaning across the table inching closer and closer to Ethan. "No." I shook my head. "No, I'm not. I'm just . . ."

"Hungry," Ethan said quickly.

"Yes. I mean no." I sat back, frustrated, my dark hair falling into my eyes like a shroud of misery. "I just . . . haven't had a burger in years."

"You haven't?" Cindy bit into a fry. "Why not?"

Think quick, Scarlet! "Oh . . . you know. My parents are . . .

they're . . . vegetarians." It wasn't a lie. When vampires resort to sucking blood from animals, it's considered being a vegetarian. Hey, I never said we were vegans.

Ethan snorted like he knew something more about me than he let on. "Vegetarians . . . eh?"

The incident in the forest probably didn't help the situation. I guess I hadn't been as clever as I thought. "Yeah." I balled my hand in a fist. "What's it to you, dog face?"

Cindy's gaze darted between me and Ethan.

"Nothing." Ethan struggled not to snarl, his lips doing this weird dance. "Never mind."

Yeah, that's what I thought.

Chapter 16

When Saturday morning came Mort and Drac didn't have any objections to the school carnival. Not like they could when Cindy was already on my doorstep. Not like they noticed when I tried to give them a pathetic expression.

"These are my sisters, Winnie and Bertha." Cindy pointed to two girls standing behind her. They didn't look like her at all. I hadn't noticed them in school before, so they were probably in different classes, maybe even a different grade.

"Hi," I said with an awkward smile.

A man standing behind her cleared his throat.

Cindy rolled her eyes. "Oh, and this is my dad. Roger."

"Nice to meet you, Scarlet. I've heard lots about you." He shook my hand. Then he reached in the doorway, sticking his hand out for my parents. "Mr. . . . Mrs. Small . . . ?"

"Nice of you to take Scarlet to the carnival for us," Drac said formally. He was so stiff sometimes.

"Yes, yes," Mort's cheerful attitude was hard to miss as she took Roger's hand.

"Of course." Roger seemed like a nice guy. Cindy was so lucky to have an awesome dad. "And this is my wife, Hagatha."

"Really?" Mort's eyes lit with an emotion I couldn't pinpoint. "Well, I must thank you again."

"Anytime," Hagatha said. "It's our pleasure."

"You ready?" Cindy interrupted.

"Sure." Although I wasn't eager about the carnival, the parental formality really irritated me. I turned around and waved. "See you later."

"Have fun," Mort called out.

I gave her an eye-roll. She definitely didn't get the fact that this wasn't something I wanted to do.

Outside the school doors, Sarah waited for us. "Hey Chickey Monkey," Cindy said, linking arms with her. We skipped up the steps together, Winnie and Bertha following close behind. Roger and Hagatha kept their distance. While I might have been new to the whole friend thing, it felt great to be included.

"Where's Hunter?" Cindy asked Sarah.

Sarah hung her head. Any ounce of happiness faded.

"Oh." Cindy put her head on Sarah's shoulder. "I'm sorry."

Sarah faked a smile.

This whole middle-school drama stuff never made sense.

"What? I mean what happened?" Secretly I sang an angelic note in my head. My chances of running into Ethan were slim.

Sarah gave me a look like I was probably the stupidest person she'd ever met.

"Hunter had stuff . . ." Cindy said, ". . . to do today. But I'm sure we'll see him later."

"You're probably right," I said chiming in. I think I might actually have sounded genuine. Maybe I actually got the hang of this fitting in thing!

The three of us shuffled into the school, arms still linked, like we were inseparable friends. Cindy waved for Winnie and Bertha to join us but they stayed a few steps behind.

The Busy Bee Carnival buzzed with loads of people playing games in various classrooms, eating food in the old gymnasium (complete with a stage) turned cafeteria, and carrying large stuffed toys under their arms. Ethan stood in front of the beanbag toss game. I didn't need to see him to know because I smelled his dogginess from two blocks away.

Ethan reached out his hand to Cindy and she practically skipped to him. As soon as they were side by side, he put his arm around her shoulder and turned back, snarling. I wanted to hiss at him, but I didn't. Mostly for my old suckers. I needed to be on my best behavior even if it double killed me.

Winnie and Bertha ambled up to my side, taking my hand and pulling me along. Their warm hands were a shock to my icy skin and I gasped. Even though a brief moment of surprise flashed on their faces, they didn't say anything about it. They were a weird bunch and I wondered what was up with that family. They were almost as strange as my own!

Ethan hovered over Cindy. He made me want to cringe. Or kill him. Probably both. I hated werewolves and there was nothing that wolf-boy could ever do to win my trust.

Ethan guided Cindy through a maze of yellow and black balloons. "How clever," I mumbled. "Like fat bumble bees." I didn't really think it was clever. I thought it was lame. Just like all the other times I'd seen it.

Winnie laughed. "Bertha was on the decorating committee."

"Wuzzzz not," Bertha buzzed.

Winnie crossed her eyes.

"Okay. Fine. I was," Bertha admitted. "But I didn't have any say in the decorations. I just helped fill the balloons with helium."

Ms. Lily stood on the stage and tapped a microphone. "Attention, attention." She cleared her throat. "Is this thing on?" As her voice streamed in over the loud speaker, the room quieted. "Ah!" Her eyes grew wide with excitement as she heard her voice over the noise of the carnival. "Five minutes until the pie-eating contest. Registration is at the front of the stage." She sank into an oversized chair behind the registration table. Within seconds she dozed off, her mouth agape, lightly snoring. People began chatting loudly.

Ethan stopped in his tracks and lifted his nose in the air, sniffing. "Pie? Did someone say pie?" He glanced around. "Who's with me?" he asked.

Winnie shook her head. Cindy and Sarah giggled. Bertha shrugged and I could tell she wanted to chow down on a bunch of pies. She must have had a sweet tooth just like me.

"I'll do it," I said. If I excelled at anything, it was eating and eating fast. Vampires are good at a fast kill.

VAMPIRE RULE #28
Fast food is our specialty: kill, eat, and run!

Sure, fast food normally involves sucking blood (not a drive-thru), but I like real food too. Whoever says vampires don't eat real food obviously doesn't know any vampires. It's just not very nutritious for us and doesn't fill us up.

Besides, I wasn't going to give Ethan a chance to beat me at anything.

Ethan dodged the crowd as he led the way toward the stage. But there was no way I would be led by a dog, so I pushed past him and everyone followed me instead.

I marched straight up to the registration desk. "Scarlet. Scarlet Small," I said slamming my palms onto the table.

Ms. Lily woke with a start. "Pie-eating contest?" she asked.

I wanted to say something sarcastic. What else would I be standing in line for? "Um, yeah," I said, being good instead. In fact, I'd say a halo floated over my head.

Once I put my name and address on a card Ms. Lily pinned a number onto my shirt. Twelve.

Ethan got number thirteen—my lucky number.

Great. So much for that. Now I'd have to permanently change my lucky number from thirteen to something else. Preferably like two thousand gazillion. Anything as far away as possible from Ethan and his thirteen.

I really hoped I wouldn't have to sit next to Ethan during the contest. If I did, I'd have to try real hard at not regurgitating. Which meant I would have to plug my nose because I was sure that if his doggy smell didn't get the better of me, I could win this thing.

Only one more person signed up for the pie contest after Ethan, the principal, Mr. G. Petto. Between creepy Mr. Petto and Ethan's doggy smell, I was a goner. What was I thinking?

Ms. Lily picked up the microphone. "Pie contest starts in T-minus sixty seconds. Fifty-nine. Fifty-eight. Fifty-seven. Fifty-six—"

Mr. Petto grabbed Ms. Lily's sleeve. She covered the microphone, leaned down toward him, listening as he grunted something in her ear.

Ms. Lily stood up and cleared her throat. "Apparently a countdown isn't necessary," she said blushing. "Contestants, please take your place on stage."

Unfortunately, they filed us into a line in numerical order. I sat down on a hard metal chair. Ethan plopped on the chair to my right. His doggy smell drifted up my nose. Great.

A scrawny girl with braces and greasy hair sat to my left. The girl's long braids brushed the pie in front of her. For a second I wondered if one of her hairs fell in her pie, maybe she'd get grossed out and quit the contest. But I realized

that it didn't really matter. She was scrawny. How many pies could she eat anyway?

With everyone situated, Ms. Lily started a timer. She blew her whistle.

Everyone on stage plunged into their pies. But for some reason, I couldn't bring the dish to my face, or my face to it. My throat choked up like a hair-clogged drain.

What was wrong with me?

Screaming voices and cheering fans all blended together in one muffled sound. The audience seemed to be in slow motion and all the noise drifted thousands of miles away. It felt as though I was the only one in the room. I think they say that's what happens right before you pass out. Good thing my vision didn't go black.

Cindy jumped up and down, her mouth opening and closing as she cheered. Winnie, Bertha, and Sarah threw fists to the sky calling out something that sounded like "Scar-than." So I didn't know if they were chanting for me or Ethan or both. It didn't really matter, because even if they were chanting for me, I was probably already two pies behind everyone else.

The other messy-faced contestants devoured their pies.

All of this was probably Ethan's fault. His furry-self probably shed on my clothes, giving me a real-life fur ball! I swallowed hard and forced that fur-ball-lump to the pit of my stomach. I finally brought the pie to my face. Even though I'd been able to smell the sweetness (despite Ethan's icky odor), filling my head with its sugary goodness, it really hit me as I brought it right under my nose.

And it smelled sweet. And warm. And . . .

I remembered the pies Mort used to bake when I was little. Long before I was a vampire. Drac loved pies so Mort baked one every day. It would come out of the oven and fill the entire house with its aroma. Steam would float off it when she placed it on the windowsill to cool. Mort would cut a slice and whisper, "Drac will never notice." She'd place the plate, with a single slice, on the table and we'd laugh as we shared bites until it was all gone and we were longing for more. Those pies were sweet and sugary and they filled my belly with a warm happiness.

Of course now I realize it's impossible not to notice a slice of pie is missing. So I knew Drac was aware of our scheming, but like a good father, he never said anything. He'd just smile and say, "Hmmm . . . pie." I also knew that even though those pies were delicious, there was nothing better than those shared moments with Mort.

The ball of fur returned to my throat and my eyes flooded with tears, making my face wet. I didn't want to think about things that hurt . . . because thinking of those days made me sad. I missed them so much.

I swiped away the tears, hoping no one noticed.

Then I plunged my face into the pie.

It filled my mouth and I tried not to notice if it tasted sweet because I really wanted it to be bitter. Maybe I wouldn't be reminded of the past anymore. I was too stubborn to let old memories take control.

I gobbled up the pie faster than I ever thought I could. As hard as I tried not to taste its sweetness—its subtle vanilla flavor—it flooded my taste buds, turning my mouth into a saliva-filled Niagara Falls.

I ate and ate until the pie vanished. I reached for another dish. I ate it just as quickly as the first. A judge, with a great-big-humungo smile like he was super pleased with my performance, placed a third pie in front of me. I chomped down into the crust, tasting its salty flakiness. Followed by the filling. Cherry. Yummy, delicious cherry . . . just like Mort used to make. And instead of the bitterness I longed for I became jam-packed with a warmth that filled my stomach until I felt like I'd burst.

The pies were so good—I never enjoyed real food like this. I was happy. I felt like maybe I belonged here. Maybe Cindy and Sarah were my friends. Real friends.

Filled with happiness, I dove into my fourth pie. I chomped and chewed and slurped until I was covered in goopy, red syrup. Out of the corner of my eye I saw that Ethan had only wolfed down three pies. I could beat that dog-boy and maybe even win this thing! I was so excited I started smiling. And because I was so excited and happy, my adrenaline kicked in.

And adrenaline kicking in means one thing to vampires. FANGS.

Chapter 17

I couldn't control it any longer. My undead heart felt happy, emotions flooded me, and I had no control over them. My fangs popped out!

VAMPIRE RULE #154

Don't get excited when you think you might be winning. Excitement means fangs. And fangs aren't good. Especially in a room full of non-vampires. Especially when you should be minding your manners. You know, rule #3 and all that.

No, no, no! No fangs! Not now!

But even though my brain screamed for the fangs to go away, I grinned like a fool. A stupid, cherry-faced fool! Bright red pie filling covered my face and dripped down my shirt. And I smiled.

A bright red cherry-faced smile.

A bright red, cherry-faced, vampire-fanged smile.

Some people in the front row began to stare. I probably looked like a crazed lunatic.

But stupid me, I couldn't take my eyes off them and I stared back. I couldn't close my mouth or make my eyes stop popping out of my head. So I did the only thing I knew how to do in that kind of situation. I continued smiling.

A bright red, syrup-dripping, white-fanged, crazy-eyed smile.

The people staring nudged a few of the people around them. And they began staring too! Some of them gasped. A lot of them pointed. But most of them just dropped their jaws in shock.

Oh, no! People were staring.

Stop smiling! Go away fangs!

My undead heart leapt in my chest. If that kept up, I might come back to life at any moment.

Go away, go away, go away! Now's not the time to blow your cover!

In some sort of desperation to make those stupid fangs go away, I ran my tongue across them. I smacked my lips.

Lip-smacking, cherry-syrup-dripping, white-fanged, crazy-eyed smile.

A gawking audience gaped back.

In the front row, Cindy's dad, Roger, looked ill. His face went pale as a ghost, his lips white, as if he'd eaten a powdered donut. He squeaked out a mousy-little scream. He suddenly looked as if he were teetering on a tightrope. His

knees buckled. Before anyone could catch him, Cindy's dad fainted.

Cindy and Hagatha rushed to his side. Winnie and Bertha caught up a second later. They knelt there, shaking his shoulder and calling his name. Roger remained on the floor, limp and lifeless. Just like my recent meal.

A chorus of screams rang out. Maybe because people were aware of the half-dead man in the cafeteria, or maybe because I looked like a hot vampire mess in a room full of potential victims.

It wasn't just women who screamed and shrieked. Oh no, men were hollering, too, like squealing, grunting pigs. Just like my last human-hunt with the old suckers. Good times, good times. Except I was pretty sure my parents wouldn't be happy about this. There was enough noise to wake the dead. Plus, I'm pretty sure they'd have my head when they learned I'd revealed our secret.

The room looked like a bee hive—everyone buzzing. Except their motions were crazy and absent-minded with no real direction. Some tried to help Cindy's poor, half-dead father lying on the gymnasium floor. But the rest just scrambled away from the vampire in the room.

A girl with a ponytail took out a cell phone, aiming the camera at me, but it got knocked from her hand and crashed to the floor.

Just great Scarlet.

Not only did I manage to blow my cover to one person, but I succeeded in revealing my vampire status to a room full of middle-schoolers, their parents, siblings, and the entire faculty at Charles Perrault Middle School.

So basically the entire town knew. Underworld, here I come.

A heavy-set lady rushed over to Roger, pushing Cindy aside. "I'm a nurse! I'm a nurse!" she called out. "Let me through!"

"Please help," I heard Hagatha say.

The nurse lifted his wrist. "There's a pulse, he'll be fine."

"Thank heavens," Cindy said.

The nurse pulled something from her purse, snapped it open and waved it under Roger's nose. He roused slowly, rubbed his eyes, and glanced around at his surroundings. His gaze drifted to the stage as if he'd suddenly remembered what had happened. When he saw me gawking at him, with a cherry-pie-filling-that-looked-like-blood-dripping fanged smile, he promptly fainted again.

I pushed my chair back, ready to leap off the stage. But something held me back.

I watched helplessly as people raced through the doors, pushing and shoving each other. They trampled the decorations in the process. It was all-out mayhem!

Cindy had a look on her face. Not one of surprise, but more like something that said she'd seen this before. "Don't worry," she said to anyone who would listen, "He does this all the time. He'll be okay in a few minutes."

Mr. Petto urged his secretary to call an ambulance anyway. Ms. Lily pushed her way past the crowd through the double doors and headed in the direction of the main office. No one seemed to pay her any mind as they continued to rush around in chaos.

Everyone except a short, round, little old lady, with a pair of spectacles perched atop her nose, who sat as still as a picture staring back at me.

I hadn't noticed her earlier, but then again, I hadn't noticed a lot of things.

The little old lady was easy to spot, however. The quiet amongst the storm.

Embarrassed, I surveyed the mess—pie crust that resembled human flesh and cherry juice like blood—and couldn't help but think I was no better than a horror movie because I'd effectively abolished those pies the same way a monster destroys a city.

No wonder Cindy's Dad fainted. The table looked like a massacre—and I was the ax-wielding maniac, fangs, flesh, appetite and all.

The little old lady tapped her fingers on the edge of the table. She leaned over a moment and I couldn't help but notice her beautiful curly, gray hair. It wasn't exactly gray, but more of a shimmering silver, all shiny and beautiful in the glow of the fluorescent lights. She wore a neatly pressed floral dress with a ruffled collar and a clean, white apron trimmed with lace. When she sat up I noticed her round, red cheeks and a nose to match. She appeared so friendly and lively. Almost like she could pass for Mrs. Claus.

She removed her spectacles, pulled a handkerchief from

her apron pocket and wiped cherry juice from the lenses. The granny-lady placed the glasses back on her face and tapped them at the corner once, twice, three times as if she were hammering them into place.

The granny held up a can of vegetable juice, popped it open and held it mid-air as if she were waiting to make a toast. My mouth gaped. Why wasn't she afraid? And why on earth would she be toasting me? With what looked like a Bloody Tom?

"EVERYONE, PLEASE CALM DOWN," came Mr. Petto's voice over the loud speaker. "STAY CALM. EVERYTHING IS ALL RIGHT."

"Scarlet," Ethan said, drawing my attention back to the great big mess I'd made of everything. He'd been quiet up until now. But as he yanked on my shirt, I realized he'd been holding onto my arm the whole time. "Scarlet. What did you do?"

What had I done?! WHAT HAD I DONE? Well, that was easy. I'd blown my cover, made a great-big-mess of things and the old suckers would be infuriated when they found out. We'd have to move, I'd hear about it for eternity—and not in a good way that people laugh and joke over silly events— no, this would go down in infamy as the time Scarlet Small created bedlam and ruined everything. It would be a guilt I'd have to live with forever. And ever. Like a humongous pimple that never goes away, just throbs and reminds you of its existence and its never-ending intent to ruin you.

The worst part was that we'd only been here a few days.

And I just started making friends and fitting in. So much for thinking I could stay here forever.

There was no recovering from a mess like this!

Chapter 18

I shook my head. "I . . . I . . . uh . . . don't know," I stuttered, scared and confused, and unable to take my eyes off the granny-lady.

The lady took a satisfied sip and placed the can on the table. She patted the corner of her mouth with her handkerchief, folded it neatly and placed it back in her purse.

She was all alone. No one seemed to notice—or care for that matter—that she even existed. I rubbed my eyes. Maybe I was the only one who could see her.

As if she read my mind, the little old lady looked right at me—stared through me—with a wide, crooked-toothy-white smile that seemed to whisper she needed a friend. She stood up, her weak legs trembling beneath her, and hobbled awkwardly through the side door marked with an emergency exit sign.

Oddly, an alarm never sounded, but with all the commotion, I doubt anyone would have noticed anyway.

"You scared half the town!" Ethan growled, slamming his hands on the table.

I jumped. "What? I mean . . . who me?" I tried to act blameless, making my voice high and sweet, but it was too late. Everyone knew my vampire secret. And everyone, including Ethan, knew I was guilty. "I didn't do anything." A large, sticky glop of pie dripped from my face and splattered onto the table.

"Then why are people screaming and staring at you? Cindy's dad fainted and I'm pretty sure it was your fault!"

I stared blankly at him, unable to speak. There was nothing I could say.

"Look at you! You, with all that cherry juice and those fake vampire fangs!" Ethan leaned closer, investigating. "Boy, those suckers sure do look real!"

I wanted to cry. Everything swirled around in my head, like a giant whirlpool sucking me down a dark, sad, miserable drain. A drain straight to the Underworld where I would die a most painful undead death. I was the big, bad problem. Cherry juice, blood, fake fangs, half-dead dad of my newest and only friend.

"But . . . but . . ." I tried to speak . . . but I didn't know what I wanted to say, or if I wanted to say anything at all. I just wanted it all to go away. Pretend it never happened.

Ethan's grip on my arm grew tight. "Boy," he repeated. "Those suckers sure do look real."

Wait a second. Did he just say what I thought he said?

"Did . . . you say . . . fake? Fake fangs?"

"Yeah, those faaaake fangs." He emphasized the 'fake' part, drawing out the 'a' vowel like there were hundreds of them instead of just one.

My eyes must have popped out of my head because he smiled mischievously and whispered, "Go with it Scarlet. I've got you covered."

My mortal enemy wanted to protect me? Ethan was just about the strangest boy I'd ever met.

He nodded in the direction of the gawking audience. "Hurry, before this gets worse." He squeezed my arm again, but not in a mean way. It was like one of those squeezes your parents give you when you're hurt or sad. Almost like a hug. . .

I blinked—one large, slow bat of the eyelashes. "Right. Fake. Of course." The words came out robotically because I was in disbelief. Something suddenly dawned on me. "Wait a minute . . ." I turned to Ethan in surprise. "You mean you knew?"

"Knew about those fake fangs? Sure, I watched you put them in, remember?"

What was wrong with me? He knew! He knew all along that I was a vampire. Of course he knew. He probably saw my non-reflection in his fork prongs at lunch. Probably sensed that I really wanted to eat that squirrel in the forest.

But why on earth was I questioning him? In public no less. I banged the palm of my hand against my forehead.

"Stupid. Stupid." Why hadn't he told anyone my secret? And why didn't he try to kill me when he had the chance? He could have ended my undead life in the forest, but he didn't.

I suppose none of that mattered now. I had a way out of that horrible mess. And it was all because of wolf-boy. Weird, strange, inexplicable wolf-boy.

Relieved and nervous all at once I grinned, careful not to show my fangs. "As a matter of fact, they're getting kind of annoying. Let me take them out." I turned away, calming myself so the fangs would retract. Acting like I removed a pair of Halloween fangs from my mouth, I pretended to slip them in my pocket. Good thing greasy-haired girl was passed out cold, face first in her pie. I mean, poor girl.

While the audience stood gawking, I straightened and turned to Ethan. My smile beamed showing him my non-vampire-teeth, just as if I were at the dentist. Except this was less painful. Sort of.

"So, now that we've taken care of that." Ethan threw an arm around my shoulder in a half-hug, his wet-dogginess not smelling as terrible as it normally did. "Let's take care of the rest of this mess."

"Right." How come wolf-boy acted so nice? Wouldn't he just rather I get caught, expose my vampire status, and have me shipped out to some Hades-forsaken town in the middle of nowhere? Or tell Mort and Drac so they could send me to the Underworld. He could go on with his werewolf life without any distractions from me. "So where do we start?" I asked.

Ethan pointed to the towels draped over the back of our chairs. "Clean up."

"Right." I suddenly felt very dumb and not much like a vampire who'd been around for over a hundred years. But it's not exactly like I was used to this sort of thing either. I'd never been roped into a pie-eating contest before, and I'd certainly never shown my teeth in public. Well, not since last month, precisely one hundred and twenty four years after my conversion. Hey, I'm a slow learner, okay?

Cindy ran up on stage. Oh, no. I'd forgotten she'd seen the whole vampire-cherry-pie-slaughter. I couldn't lose my new friend. My only friend. Well . . . except for Sarah. And maybe that wolf-boy. Maybe.

"Are you okay?" She rubbed my shoulder and peered straight into my eyes. Something about the way Cindy looked at me, demanded my attention. I never liked looking people in the eye, it made me squirmy and uncomfortable, like they could read all my thoughts and secrets. But when Cindy did it, I could tell it was because she really cared.

The tension in my shoulders relaxed, relieved in an odd sort of way. "Yeah, I'm fine."

She threw her arms around my neck and squeezed tight. "You had this expression on your face—this 'oh-no-I've-been-caught-and-everyone-knows-my-secret' kind of look."

"Nah, no secrets here." My chest ached a bit for lying to her.

She glanced down at her white t-shirt, now stained cherry-red from our hug. "Let's get out of here. I need a clean shirt." She eyed my pie-covered, cherry-stained, made-a-mess-of-everything clothes. "Looks like you could use a change, too."

"Yeah. Looks like it." My shirt was the least of my troubles. "I can't leave without taking care of this mess."

Ethan stopped in the middle of wiping the table "Go on," he said, practically pushing me away.

"Thanks," I said, feeling grateful as I made my first ever sincere eye-contact with wolf-boy. He returned the smile, then bent down, returning to his work. Behind him the emergency exit sign glowed. It flashed off and on, the light sputtering. Then the cafeteria went dark.

Chapter 19

The remaining people broke out into a chorus of shrieks and wails.

"No need to worry," Mr. Petto shouted above the crowd. "Just a fuse."

"Hold on Cindy." I said, my mind in a daze. "I need to take care of . . . something first." In the darkness, it was difficult to see, but I pushed through the crowd, which seemed to be frozen in fear, toward the emergency exit that glowed an eerie red.

Halfway to the door the lights popped on. Relieved sighs sounded all around me. The emergency exit door swung open and the granny-lady appeared. My pulse quickened. Had she been waiting for me?

I pushed and shoved and the granny's eyes sparkled. I needed to reach her, to talk to her, even if it was just to make sure she was real and not a figment of my imagination.

I'm coming, I thought. Wait for me.

Stepping and moving, ducking and weaving, I inched my way through the maze of people. Finally, I reached the emergency exit!

I turned right, then left, whirling in a circle . . . but the granny was gone! Where could she have disappeared to?

A tap on my shoulder caused me to jump nearly out of my skin.

"C'mon. I'll walk you home." Cindy started for the door, but when I didn't move, she stopped. "Are you all right?"

"What?" The need to find the granny-lady had overridden my common sense. "I mean. Yeah. Yeah, sure." All I wanted was a moment to talk to granny-lady, make sure she was real, but I didn't get that chance. "That would be great."

Roger pulled on his coat. "I'm sure your parents are wondering about you."

He was right. We'd been gone quite a while.

When we got to my house, Mort waited at the door, arms crossed, one foot tapping impatiently. "Thanks for bringing her home," Mort said in a fake polite way. I couldn't understand what brought on her sudden mood change. She seemed so happy to meet Cindy's parents before. Then I glanced down at my sticky shirt and thought I might know the reason for Mort's attitude.

"Not a problem. You know, Scarlet's welcome . . . anytime," Roger said as he scratched his head. Was he sincere or just being polite?

"I do appreciate that," Mort said as she steered me into the house.

Cindy must have noticed the tension because she gave a single awkward wave and ran off.

"Bye," I called after her weakly. "See you Monday." My throat tightened, choking off my words. Out of the corner of my eye, I noticed Mort's scowl. Maybe she was mad that I was late. That's all. Or upset that I'd ruined my clothes. She hates when I do that. One time I dribbled grape juice on a new sweater and you'd think that Hitler had invaded Stalingrad.

There was no way she'd heard about the fangs already.

Drac sat in his chair, his back tall and straight. Perfect posture just as an officer should. "How was the school fun fair?" he asked without bothering to turn in my direction.

My clothes clung to my body like a wet swimsuit and all I wanted was to clean up. "Um, it was good." My fingers stuck to my hair as I brushed a strand out of my face. "Same ole, same ole. You know. Games and prizes, and . . ." My stomach gurgled. ". . . a pie-eating contest."

"So I see." Mort observed my stained clothes, her arms still crossed.

"And so I hear." Drac cleared his throat and sat up taller, if that was even possible. "I understand you made quite a mess."

Uh oh. My hands trembled. He hadn't even looked at me. How did he know? "I . . . uh . . ."

"You'll need to take care of this." Drac stood up, straightening his uniform. "Mr. Petto could use an extra set of hands." Drac stepped to the side, revealing Mr. G. Petto sitting in a chair in the corner of the room.

I gasped. My time here was expired. I was a goner. Kaput.

"Why yes. Yes I could." Mr. Petto drew his hands close to his chin strumming his fingers against each other.

My undead heart leapt in my chest. This was super bad news. It meant he'd told my parents everything. Including how I screwed up. Royally. An acidic bubble rose in my throat, burning from the inside out. He probably even told the old suckers how the entire town was nearly scared to death by a cherry-pie-adoring vampire. Maybe he'd even mentioned how I managed to cover up the mistake because of a werewolf.

Wait! That was it! All I had to do was tell them about the fake fangs. Then all would be forgiven.

But not now. I couldn't mention the part about the werewolf in front of Mr. Petto. I'd have to tell them later, when things had settled a little . . . maybe after they had a little less steam coming out their ears. When it was safe for them to know all the details.

Mr. Petto stalked in my direction. He didn't stop until he was in my face, the tips of his shoes touching my cherry covered combat boots. "How about you come back to the school now and I won't give you detention? Again."

I shrunk back. My parents didn't know about the first time I'd gotten detention.

"The small riot you caused left quite a mess behind. The least you can do is help to clean it up."

I felt like he'd invaded my space just a little—and by just a little I mean he had no concept of personal space. It was hard to breathe with his hot air blowing in my face. Especially when his breath reeked of garlic. My head nodded. It seemed to do so without my consent. "Uh . . . okay. Sure thing."

"I'll see you at the school in ten minutes." Mr. Petto tapped his watch. "And not a minute later." He stepped away and went toward the door. I let out the breath I didn't know I'd been holding.

"I'll see you out." Mort bustling to him, her vintage black and white polka dot dress swaying with each step. She always dressed like a 1950s movie star. "No need." Mr. Petto tipped his head and revealed his creepy wooden-toothed smile. A large chunk of his combed-over hair fell into his eyes. "Ten minutes," he said pointing a threatening finger in my direction.

Mort closed the door behind him and Mr. Petto's footsteps clunked down the stairs like a log rolling over bumpy earth.

Mort stood there, her skirt swaying as she folded her arms, disappointment clouding her face. "You know this means we have to move now, don't you?"

"No, no we don't. I'll fix it. I promise! I'll make it better and no one will ever know the truth." I lowered my head, bangs falling into my eyes. "Besides I'm sure everyone thinks

it was a joke." Truth was, I couldn't be sure, but the fake fangs were a good cover.

Mort turned her back and her voice softened in a defeated way. "Scarlet, some things just can't ever be repaired."

Chapter 20

Mort didn't scream or shout the way I thought she would. Instead she sighed, long and deep, like she'd never find the end of her disappointment. I felt so small. And not just because of my last name. A different kind of small, like I was the worst thing on the planet.

"You've let us down, Scarlet," Drac said. He went into the kitchen, opened the fridge and poured a Bloody Tom. He sat on a bar stool on the other side of the counter and stuck a celery stalk into his drink. He swirled it like the celery knew his thoughts and would give him answers.

My heavy heart sank. "I know I did. And I'm really . . ." Sorry, I thought. But there was no point in saying it. Sorry wouldn't change anything now. If there was anything worse than angry parents, it was disappointed ones. I'd have to find a way to fix this, but now wasn't the time. I had to go to the school first and help Mr. Petto clean the cafeteria.

Without changing my clothes, or even bothering to wash up, I dragged myself out the door, closing it quietly behind me. My head sagged so low it felt like my chin might scrape along the sidewalk.

Cheer up, Scarlet. You'll fix it. You will. You have to. If you don't then you're doomed to the Underworld.

At the school, there were only a few people, mostly parents, still helping with clean up. When they saw me, they turned away and mumbled to each other.

"She's a bad influence," one of them whispered.

"Not to my daughter," another griped back. "I'll make sure she keeps her distance."

My chest felt tight. If people were going to talk behind my back, at least they could do it without my knowledge.

"Well, well." Mr. Petto bowed, sweeping his arm across his body into the open room. "Our little star has arrived."

"I'm not a star," I mumbled. Little did he know I bowed in return. In my head.

Mr. Petto narrowed his eyes. "What's that? Were you talking back?"

"No sir." My back straightened automatically. "I . . . I just want to help clean up. I'll mop the stage," I said, the messy hardwood floors catching my eye. I knew I'd made a mess, but I had no idea of how bad it looked from a distance. Cherry juice and pie crust covered the floor with more bits and pieces splattered on the walls. It looked like a slaughter house.

Dragging the mop behind me, I lumbered up the stairs of the stage. My feet stuck to the floor with every step, but before long all the evidence vanished. When I finished, I admired my work. The floor shined clean as a whistle. Satisfied, I took a few steps toward the door.

Principal Petto came up behind me and tapped my shoulder. "Where do you think you're going?"

"Nowhere," I said, my dusty, rotten heart skipping a beat. I don't know why this guy bothered me so much. He was just a stupid human, a principal of a school who carved wood in his spare time. If he was a security guard I would have made a snack of him. "I was just making sure I did I good job."

"Well." He handed me a cloth. "You can admire your work as you wipe down the tables."

I don't know why, but I felt like a submissive child. Granted, to him I was still a child. But trust me, I had plenty more years of experience in this world, even if they did come in the form of a hundred-year-old trapped in a twelve year old vampire body.

Without a sound, I made my way across the room to the first row of tables directly in front of the stage. A bucket sat in the center waiting for me to put it to good use. Wringing out the cloth I began to scrub away, wiping up pieces of pie and splatters of juice.

As I washed, reaching for a particularly stubborn stain, I stubbed my foot on the leg of the table. I bent down to nurse my aching toe and spied a neatly folded slip of paper.

A vision flashed in my head. Granny-lady had sat in this seat. She'd been so calm as she wiped her lenses clean. Had she been the one to drop this piece of paper?

My hand trembled as I reached for it. It wasn't like me to feel so nervous, especially something as insignificant as a piece of paper. Mr. Petto had been on my case a bit too much, (even if I deserved some of it) so that must have shot my nerves.

The paper was inches from my grasp and my heart beat so loud it pounded in my ears. Calm down. It was probably nothing. A receipt from someone's wallet. A note passed between friends. Maybe even a homework assignment.

Still, I needed to know what was on it. I couldn't help but think that the granny-lady had dropped it . . . and maybe she had done so in hopes that I'd find it. I stretched, reaching for it, eager to see the writing that lay within the page.

"Scarlet!" a voice called. "What is that?"

I grabbed the paper and crumpled it into my palm. As I stood up, I smacked the back of my head on the edge of the table.

"What is that?" Ms. Lily stood across the room pointing in my direction.

My heart pounded as I shoved the paper in my pocket. "What are you talking about, Ms. Lily?"

She pointed at me. "That. That right there!"

The paper seemed to beat with every frantic cobweb-laden heartbeat and living-impaired breath I took. "I . . . uh . . . don't know what you're talking about." A bead of sweat trickled down, reaching the corner of my eye, seeping in until it stung so bad my eyes watered.

Ms. Lily marched, her arm still extended like her finger was a guided missile. "You most certainly do. You know exactly what I'm talking about." She shook her finger as if she were scolding a toddler. "That Ms. Scarlet . . . is . . ."

"Is . . .?" My body trembled like a leaf in a windstorm. My face was a mess of sweat, teary-eyes and drippy nose.

". . . is a great job." She lowered her arm. "You'd never know there was a pie-eating contest here today." Ms. Lily strolled closer and patted my back. "Nice work."

Phew! Close one. Thank goodness she didn't notice the paper. "Thanks." A grin spread across my lips as I wiped the sweat from my forehead with the back of my sleeve.

"Now why don't you go home and clean yourself up." Her ruffled skirt swung in place as she spoke, like it were an extension of her body. "You've done all you can here." Ms. Lily looked so sweet and calm, I almost felt better.

"Okay." I nodded, curling my fingers tightly around the paper in my pocket.

"See you Monday," Ms. Lily said as she strolled away.

I felt silly for being so uptight and letting my emotions control me, instead of controlling them the way I'd been taught to do.

VAMPIRE RULE #96

Control your emotions. Otherwise you're just looking for trouble.

When Ms. Lily was out of sight, I dashed through the emergency exit door—the same door the granny-lady had disappeared through. I collapsed against the closed door, relieved.

The slip of paper called to me. Maybe it contained magical, wonderful words written just for me that would tell me how to make everything better and remind me that I'm not alone.

I unfolded the edges, careful not to tear it. My corporeal-challenged breath caught in my throat. Another fold and all would be revealed! Inside that folded piece of paper was music. A staff of music with its accompanying lyrics.

"Over the river and through the woods . . ." I spoke the words under my breath.

That's it? A stupid piece of music? That's the wisdom on this meaningless scrap of paper?

The cold blood coagulating in my veins boiled. My face lit on fire. My fist curled around the sheet music, crumpling it into a tight little wad. "I'll 'over the river and through the woods' right on top of that stupid piece of paper." I threw it as hard as I could, but it floated softly to the ground. That only irritated me further and I didn't even try to resist the urge to stomp on it. My boot slammed down hard in a child-like fit of rage. "Stupid paper. Stupid song." I danced on that paper until my legs ached. "Stupid paper, stupid song . . . stupid me!"

Exhausted, I sank to the ground. Wrapping my arms around my legs, I pressed my back against the brick wall of

the school. "How could I be so dumb?" Tears rolled down my cheeks. "Why did I think a piece of paper would help me?"

My life was over. Everything sucked. It was the worst vampire bite ever.

The tears continued to flow. I couldn't believe how I'd messed up everything. No one would trust me ever again. We'd have to move, or worse, I'd have to go labor for an eternity in the Underworld.

The sky grew dark as the sun set in the distance. The moon rose high above the treetops. I noticed how shadows danced against the building. They teased the trees. Even the green grass glowed an incredible shade of turquoise. As mad as they were, my parents would probably come searching for me soon.

The cold cement chilled my already icy and lifeless body. For the first time in my afterlife, my bones began to ache. I pulled my thin shirt tighter around me. But it was damp and sticky and I was still covered in cherry juice.

The sky glittered with stars and I wished things could have been different. If only I could be different. If only . . .

Trees in the dense woods, swayed to the rhythm of a song as a familiar tune echoed in the air. I hummed along, the beautiful bell-like tones soothing me.

Words seemed to come to my mind as though they were part of me from long ago.

". . . to grandmother's house we go . . . the horse knows the way . . ."

My hands drifted into the air, floating, as though they were conducting an unseen orchestra.

"... to carry the sleigh ... through the white and drifted snow ..."

Thoughts came to my mind and I slowly stood, my legs wobbling beneath me. Whether it was fear or excitement I wasn't sure.

"... Over the river and through the wood ..."

I stopped, my hands dropping at my side, my body frozen.

"Over the river and through the wood." The words came softly from my mouth as though they had a mind of their own.

"Over the river and through the wood ..."

A recognition washed over me. Could it be?

My eyes darted to the paper, still in a balled up heap, just a few feet away from me. Only moments earlier I'd stomped on that paper out of anger. I'd thought it was ridiculous. The paper seemed to have meaning and purpose now.

I reached for it, unfolding its hard lines and smoothing it against the pavement. Sure enough, the words were there. Over the river and through the woods.

"To grandmother's house we go," I sang in a hushed tone.

If that granny-lady had left this paper, then it was certainly intended for me. I just knew it, without a doubt. And if she'd left it for me, then I had no choice.

To grandmother's house I would go.

Chapter 21

Putting one shaky foot in front of the other, I braved the forest. You'd think being a vampire would make me courageous and bold. Don't let the vampire status fool you. I was still terrified of all the things lurking in the woods. Mort had nearly scared me into a second afterlife with all her crazy werewolf stories. In her tales they were always in the forest.

My mind raced. Ethan!

Maybe he'd been nice during the pie-eating contest, but there was no telling what he'd do when he was in true form. Werewolves were so unpredictable and moody.

In the distance, a glow of lights seemed to brighten, lighting the woods so the outline of trees only served to remind me how very suffocating they felt. Woods hugged all around me, like a blanket on a sick child.

The light seemed to breathe, growing stronger one minute and dimming the next, but never going out.

It must be her house, I thought. It had to be.

But what if it wasn't? What would happen to me then? This was a stupid idea.

If I didn't go, though, I would never know. Besides, I could turn around any time I felt like it. The granny-lady didn't need to know if I backed out, if I got too scared. She could just think I never saw her note.

That would be okay, right?

Despite the glow in the distance, I wished I had a flashlight. It would make me feel safer. I kicked myself for ignoring yet another rule.

VAMPIRE RULE #162
How many times do I have to tell you? Carry a flashlight.

My footfalls crunched on the leaves, snapping twigs with each step. The noise sounded much louder than it should. The wind howled, trees aching and creaking like an old man's knees, birds swooping overhead. It was beautiful in an eerie sort of way.

Wait . . . birds? After dark?

That couldn't be right. Birds slept at night. Except owls, of course.

This wasn't exactly what I'd hoped for when I figured out that note. The menacing woods and their creepy sounds made me anxious, my palms growing clammy with each step. Add to it the strange sight of all those birds.

I had to get out of the forest. I didn't know what lurked in the woods, or what possessed birds into crazy behavior, but I certainly didn't want to find out!

My step quickened. The school was too far behind me to go back. The only choice I had was forward to the little cottage which beckoned with its warm glow and happy music.

I pressed onward—the sound of wings still close behind—through a thicket of grass, where all sorts of living creatures dwelled. Normally I would have hunted them to satisfy my hunger and thirst. Instead I pressed forward, pushing branches and twigs out of my way. They thwapped back, scratching my face.

One of the strange birds plummeted, nearly colliding into me. At the last second, it made a sharp turn and landed on a tree branch.

"Shade?" Could it really be? "Oh Shade! Where have you been?"

He swooped down, landing on my shoulder and nestling close to my neck.

"Good boy, Shade!" I patted his head. "I thought I'd never see you again. Want to help me find my way to granny's house?" As soon as the words left my mouth, he flew away.

VAMPIRE RULE #164

Bats suck. They're stupid. And their echo-location is super-lame. It lacks vision.

"Fine, you dingbat. Who needs you anyway?" But I did. I needed him. I longed for another pet, a friend.

Uneasiness returned making my knees clang together. After nervously making my way through the forest, I came to a perfectly circular clearing, with a little cottage smack dab in the center.

I let the branches slip from my hands, and they closed behind me, like a gate shutting me out. Or perhaps locking me in.

I tiptoed toward the house. I'd heard stories about houses in the middle of the woods. Sometimes there are bears who don't like sharing their things (like porridge or their beds) and they especially don't like having their chairs broken. Or there are boys who plant magic beans that grow tall stalks leading to a giant and a gold-egg-laying goose. Though I know that last one was true. I met Jack once. Nice kid. He made out like a bandit. Deserved every penny, too, if you ask me.

But sometimes . . . sometimes those houses in the woods were occupied with witches disguised as old ladies who stuff you full of candy, just to fatten you up so they can eat you for dinner. Why didn't I think of that before?

What if Mort's stories were true? Would I be putting myself in danger? A lump formed in my throat. I didn't want to be eaten by a witch. It was a horrid way to die.

But . . . but what if Mort told me those stories just so I would be good? What if they were her way to scare me into

perfection? Then I'd stop making mistakes and be the perfect little ghoul she always wanted me to be.

Or, maybe they were true and I'd be rich once I found some magic beans and a golden-egg laying goose!

My feet wobbled beneath me as I stepped into the clearing of neatly groomed grass.

Chapter 22

Meticulously manicured flower beds surrounded the perimeter of a house that looked as if it were pasted straight from a children's picture book.

A little old lady with a friendly face sat on a bench situated under a window, her hands busy with a ball of black yarn. She knit furiously in the dim light of a lantern, completely unaware that I was watching her.

Her round face, the spectacles, the dress with neatly pressed apron. My dearly departed heart leapt in my chest. She was here! The granny-lady was here! I cleared my throat, letting her know I'd arrived.

The old lady ignored me as she continued to knit; her fingers, the needles, and the black yarn flew in a frantic display. She paused, held the work up to the moonlight and nodded approvingly. Then she placed it on her lap.

"Well, I see you found my note." She peered over the top of her glasses.

"Yes, ma'am," I said, brushing the hem of my shirt. I might be a middle-schooler, but my parents taught me manners.

VAMPIRE RULE #62
Respect your elders. Address them as sir and ma'am. Especially when your father is in the military. Or a vampire. Or both. Especially both.

"It took a while to find your place, though." I shivered thinking of my travels through the forest. My chest ached a little thinking about Shade and how he'd just flown the coop again, leaving me alone and defenseless. There was a part of me that wanted to tell her how unsure I felt. It was still hard to believe this little old granny would leave a message for me. And if she did, then why?

"I was hoping you'd figure it out. Smart girl like you ought to be able to decode a little melody." She began to hum, her voice like a sweet song I've longed to hear for years.

Using my best parent-taught manners, I said, "Thank you."

The old woman moved the knitting on the bench, smoothing it until it laid flat. She wobbled to a stand, dusted off her apron, gave a satisfied grunt, and toddled off toward her little bungalow of a house.

"Come on in," she said with a friendly little wave of her hand.

VAMPIRE RULE #170

Don't hesitate when invited into a house with a nice little old lady, even if she is a stranger. She probably has a plate of cookies and a cup of warm milk waiting for you.

I skipped inside, nearly knocking her over.

What did I have to be afraid of? Granny wasn't a stranger, now was she? She was a kind little old lady who left a note, inviting me to her place. She probably needed a friend, someone with a warm, kind heart willing to make some time for her.

Unfortunately, my heart was dead and cold, but still . . . I could be a good friend.

Besides, if it turned out she wasn't what I thought, I was a vampire. I could easily suck the life from her. And since this old lady lived in the woods, no one knew she was here, and they'd never know if she were gone.

Seriously, I had nothing to be afraid of.

"Have a seat," Granny said, pointing to a plump couch.

"Thank you." I stepped toward it, my nose filling with the scent of pies and sweets, just like Mort used to make when I was small.

A partially assembled puzzle stretched out neatly on a table, a beautiful scene of a cottage in the woods with a bridge and a pond. Trees surrounded the house like a fence, locking the beauty inside and keeping all the ugliness out. If I didn't know better, I'd almost think it was Granny's house.

But Granny's house didn't have a pond or a bridge. It was just the house, in the middle of a clearing.

Granny handed me a plate of cookies. "Help yourself, dearie."

I took one and chomped down. Gingerbread. It tasted like Christmas. I closed my eyes, remembering my childhood, the one before my vampire days. A sigh flooded my chest and I breathed deep, trying to control it. If I wasn't careful, I could have another pie massacre, except with gingerbread cookies.

"Taste good?" Granny asked sheepishly.

I nodded in agreement. This cookie, just like those pies, tasted out of this world—I almost felt like a normal human kid again. "Ummm . . . hmmm." Crumbs fell from my mouth.

"It's a recipe I found lying around my cupboards. Can you believe that? All that time I never knew!" Her plump rosy cheeks bent into a smile that made her sweet eyes squint into little slits of quarter moons.

"They're just like . . ."—more crumbs fell—". . . Mort used to make."

"Mort?"

"My mom."

"Used to make?" Granny hobbled out of the room and returned with a warm mug of milk. She handed it to me.

The fragrance of vanilla filled me with a warmth I hadn't known since I was small. "Thank you." I took a gulp, washing down the tasty remains of cookie.

Granny sat in an arm chair large enough to seat two of

her. The cushions sunk beneath her, enveloping her in soft padding and fabric. "Has your mother stopped baking for quite a while?" She squirmed a bit until she righted herself into a comfortable position.

I nodded eagerly. "Almost one hundred . . ." I nearly said 'years' but that would have been a really bad slip of the tongue! Luckily I caught myself, taking another bite of cookie and swallowing scratchy bits of it before I was ready. My chest heaved with a cough. ". . . one hundred days."

"Oh, I see," Granny said, her voice like a soft whisper. "You've really missed gingerbread cookies now, haven't you?"

"Yes, I have." How I love my gingerbread cookies. Most people use raisins for eyes on the little dough shaped men, but I hate raisins. Who likes wilted grapes anyway? So gross. Mort used licorice. Funny, so did Granny.

"Have another," Granny insisted, pushing the plate across the small wooden table between us.

I grabbed one and ate it quickly. It seemed to satisfy me in an odd sort of way. Which was very strange. Only a fresh animal meal could fill me up like that. In fact, the cookies were so good my primal instincts kicked in.

My fangs popped out!

Chapter 23

No! No, no, no! No fangs!

Thankfully, they seemed to obey my pleading and they retracted slowly. "These are the best cookies I've ever tasted."

"You seem to really enjoy sweets, don't you, dearie."

I nodded. "Yes, ma'am." That, and you know, vampire food.

"You liked those pies today, didn't you?"

I stopped mid bite, my breath catching in my throat and my heart heaving in my chest. I did love those pies. They tasted like my childhood, warm and sweet. My cheeks flushed with embarrassment.

"You've still got some of those pies on your clothes, don't you, dearie?" Granny pointed to my shirt, still covered in bright red cherry juice.

I shoved the remains of the cookie into my mouth and grabbed a third. "I didn't have much time to change. Principal Petto made me stay and clean up my mess."

"Of course, dearie. And you did it, didn't you? Just like a nice little girl."

My mouth was full of a third cookie. "Um, hum."

"I suppose those clothes feel terrible," Granny said.

My head nodded vigorously, excited that someone finally paid attention to me and understood. I took a gulp of milk, finally clearing my mouth of food. "Why yes, yes they do." Instinctively, I tugged at my shirt, letting it hang in place, still soggy and sticky.

"Well, I think I have the perfect thing for that." Granny inched her way out of the big chair, and hobbled out of the room, a blanket draped over her shoulder.

Noises sounded down the hall. Puffs of smoke billowed out into the living room. "This darned fireplace . . ." Granny said with a cough.

"Can I help you?" I called.

"No, no, dearie. Be there in a moment." Even though Granny was in the other room and I couldn't see her face, I could hear the smile in her voice.

A second later she returned with, a clean, crisp white blouse—nearly identical to my own—draped over her arm. "This should feel better."

"Oh no, I couldn't. My parents would never allow it."

"Consider it a gift. From a lonely old lady to a sweet girl."

A smile crept on my face. No one had ever shown me this much kindness. Not in my whole vampire life. In fact, most people ran the other way, especially when I exposed my fangs.

VAMPIRE RULE #70

Don't show your fangs to your so-called friends. Ever. Even if you think they'd never tell, the whole school is going to know and before you know it, the old suckers will be packing up the house and moving to another town. Trust me. I know. Past experiences and all.

"Thank you." Maybe it was wrong, but the old suckers didn't need to know. I wiped my hands on a napkin and politely took the blouse from Granny.

"Bathroom is down the hall, to the right."

I wandered through the small cottage—which seemed much larger on the inside than it did on the outside—until I reached the bathroom. My shirt was such a mess that I just dropped it on the floor as I changed into the clean one.

A moment later I went back to the living room. "A perfect fit." I twirled in a circle for Granny to see my beautiful, clean, white blouse. "Thank you so much."

Granny opened the drapes and a grayish haze of sunlight poured in through the front window, making my eyes squint. The sun was barely setting when I walked here.

"Is it morning already?" How did that happen?

Granny sat back down in her chair, picked up her ball of yarn and began knitting furiously. "Morning always comes fast."

"My parents must be worried," I thought aloud.

"Then you should probably be on your way." Granny didn't keep her gaze down. She just peered through the cloudy lenses of her spectacles and continued knitting.

"Yes." I thought about the journey home.

Outside, the sky turned from gray to a sickening cat's-eye yellow, unlike any sunrise I'd ever seen. It was just about the strangest color I'd ever seen. But maybe dawn was different in the forest, the light obstructed by the trees.

"All right, dearie." Granny reclined in her chair, waved, then calmly resumed knitting with the needles and ball of yarn in her lap. "See you soon."

I strolled toward the door and stopping a moment, I waved back. "See you tomorrow." I didn't know why I said that.

"Excellent," Granny said. "Why don't you bring a friend?"

Good idea, I thought to myself. Then I wouldn't have to walk through the forest alone.

"I'll have more treats waiting." Granny's eyes narrowed. "Special treats, just for you." Granny's face filled with such a sugary happiness, that I felt happy. I longed for another visit. Who wouldn't be grateful for an invitation from a kind old lady to visit again?

A noise, loud as thunder, sounded in the distance.

Granny seemingly perked up, but continued knitting. I didn't know what the noise was, but I certainly didn't want to find out. I stepped one foot out the door, surveying my surroundings. Even in all my vampire hunting days I'd never seen a sky so strangely colored. The only thing that had ever come close was the sky over the Atlantic Ocean when I traveled by ship from Europe to New York City, back in 1913. Although people were horrified the ship would go down like another Titanic, they were more terrified when they found dead bodies because of the vampire on board.

Other than the crashing noise somewhere deep in the woods, everything was still. I wasn't afraid of the noise, though. I was a vampire, bold, brave, strong. Well, most of the time. Well, never.

My skin prickled as I looked around nervously. The door slammed shut as I rushed home. Mort and Drac would either be infuriated, ready to punish me with the worst grounding of a vampire deathtime, or so relieved and happy they'd welcome me with open arms.

Branches slapped my face and clawed at my arms as I hurried home. Muddy clumps of soil smooshed beneath my feet. Maybe I wouldn't get lost, like the last time I'd run off.

The forest felt a little less creepy now with the sun's early morning rays to light my path, even if it was a strange sort of toxic yellow. Animals scurried through the brush, aware of the predator in their midst. Maybe that's why Shade had left. He feared I'd turn him into a snack. I couldn't blame him, really.

Oddly, the smell of all the forest animals didn't tempt me at all. I wasn't hungry for blood. My stomach felt full and satisfied. In fact, I almost felt a little dizzy, cloudy even. A soft patch of moss, under the umbrella of branches and leaves, beckoned to me.

The world spun in a hazy mist of treetops, leaves, and the flicker of morning. My eyelids became weights, shutting out the world in a slumber of darkness. I dreamt for hours, my memory dancing with visions of the cherry-pie-massacre, granny, and gingerbread cookies.

Something loud as thunder echoed within the forest and I jolted awake, suddenly terrified. Where was I? What had happened?

I sat up, inching my way to the base of the tree. Resting my head against the scratchy bark, I struggled to keep my breath steady and even. Something was in the woods. Was it Ethan? Would he bite me and end my undead life for good?

My brain felt foggy and I struggled to remember the trip to Granny's. So much had happened. Was any of it real? Or was it just a dream?

A chill swept over me and I rubbed my arms. My fingers caught the edge of my shirt and I remembered . . . The stupid pie-eating contest! Oh, no! My old suckers! They had probably enlisted the entire military in a search. How would I ever explain myself?

In the near distance, a howl.

The hairs on my arms stood on end. But then I

remembered how nice Ethan had been at the carnival. He wouldn't harm me. He was almost like a friend, wasn't he?

Leaves crunched in the distance. But with every step, they crunched louder, warning of an approaching predator.

Disoriented, but ready to run, I turned around and was face to face with a werewolf.

Chapter 24

My lifeless heart skipped a beat in my chest.

"E . . . ee . . . ee . . . Ethan . . . ?"

A growl.

"N . . . n . . . n . . . niiice Eee . . . ee . . . Ethan."

The werewolf growled and snapped. He smelled like Ethan but something wasn't quite right. I'd never seen him like this. Mort was right. Werewolves were completely unpredictable. I didn't think I'd ever understand werewolves, especially Ethan. One minute he saved my hide from the Cherry Pie Massacre and the next he tried to eat me!

"Good . . . dog . . . I mean . . . boy . . . I mean wolfie . . ."

His yellow eyes glowed.

Wait. Hadn't they been green before? Maybe it had just been my imagination.

The wolf bared his bright white teeth, his incisors almost

as sharp as mine. A growl rumbled from deep in his belly, a guttural sound that made the hairs on my arms stand on end. He snapped, biting close to my face, his fierce breath and hot drool invading my bubble. Two feet, man, two feet of personal space! Friend or foe, I wasn't about to become someone's snack.

VAMPIRE RULE #174

Personal space is vitally important. Especially when being pursued by a menacing werewolf intent on turning you into a snack.

I leapt up and ran. I wasn't sure which direction to go, but it didn't seem to matter. I just needed to outrun the wolf. Eventually I would reach safety, whether it be Granny's house or somewhere in town. Either way, I would be protected.

As I raced through the brush, daylight filtered through the treetops, flashing like strobe lights. Confused, I stumbled over a mound of dirt and rocks, falling hard. My chin smacked against a rock.

Get up, Scarlet! No time to worry about a small bruise.

I leapt up, trying hard to ignore my throbbing chin. I had to get out of the forest. Just had to reach safety before that wolf turned me into lunch!

With all my vampire might, I pushed a little harder, my feet pounding against the ground with each stride. I ran as fast as my little legs could carry me, the sound of the wolf

still close on my heels. In the distance I could make out the shape of buildings. Finally, I burst from the forest into my neighbor's backyard.

Phew! I'd made it!

Surely the wolf wouldn't expose himself in the middle of the day, in the wide open lawn, for all to see. I glanced over my shoulder. The wolf hid within the shadows, his yellow eyes aglow.

I didn't have to run anymore. There was safety now.

Breathless, I stumbled up the steps to the back door of our townhouse and peeked in a window. The lights were out in the house which meant the old suckers were probably still sleeping, even though the sky said morning had arrived hours ago.

The dated porch light shined a dull shade of orange. If they left the light on, they must have thought I'd come back. Or at least hoped for it. The old suckers really did love me with all their unbeating hearts! They wouldn't send me to the Underworld after all!

I jiggled the handle. Locked!

"Mort! Drac!" I called. Although the wolf remained a safe distance away, his yellow eyes glowing within the shadows, my nerves were a wreck. I don't care what anyone says, being chased by a werewolf is never cool, even when you're a vampire. Especially when you're a vampire. "I'm home!" My fingers nervously fumbled through my pocket, hoping to find my key before the wolf decided to take a chance and charge at me.

My hands came up empty. Darn! Why did I always leave my key at home? I just needed something to pick the lock.

The wolf howled. It was a warning. Or a call for more wolves to come. My breath caught in my throat and I pounded on the door again.

"Mooo-rt! Draa-ac!"

Still no answer. I had to try the front door. It was my only option. They must have left it open for me. They had to! I watched the wolf, my cold heart thumping in my chest. Would he chase me again?

It was a risk I had to take.

I thudded down the steps. The wolf's footfalls crunched in the leaves as he readied himself for a chase. I darted around the row of townhouses. The wolf followed, running parallel to my path, but staying in the shadows, along the edge of the trees.

I reached the front door and twisted the handle. It too was locked!

The old suckers must have thought I'd be smart enough to use the back door. That's what we'd always done in the past when someone was out late—or in trouble. But would they have known I was in trouble? Or was being out late without them enough of a concern? And if they wanted me to use the back door, why had they locked it?

I braced myself for another run-in with the wolf, as I pressed around the house to the back door, but he remained at a safe distance in the shadows, his heavy breath and footfalls following me.

As soon as I reached the back door again, climbing the steps two at a time, my eyes fell on a piece of paper taped to the door.

A note!

Was it there the whole time? Why hadn't I seen it before?

I pulled it from the window and sat down, leaning against the door. With shaky hands, I unfolded the paper. Maybe it was another note from Granny! It must have been. But how did she know . . .

The door flew open and I toppled backwards, the paper dropping from my hands.

Mort and Drac peered down at me, their arms folded as I grinned at their upside down faces. Mort grabbed my arm, pulling me up and wrapping me in a big hug. "Thank goodness you're okay."

"I'm fine, Mort." I hugged her back but pulled away when Drac gave his straight-faced-military-glare.

"Well, well." Drac tapped his foot. "Do you want to explain where you've been all night, young lady?"

Now that was irony. There was nothing young about me. But what could I tell him? I couldn't let them know about the sweet granny-lady—not after all their warnings not to talk to strangers. Certainly, I couldn't tell them about the werewolf or they'd freak out and then we'd have to move. I just started to like it here and the new friends I'd made.

"We're just glad to have you home, Scarlet." Mort tried to seem calm, but I could see her fear hiding behind that fake-smile.

"Thanks." I squeezed past my parents. "I think I'll just head to my coffin now."

"Not so fast." Mort pointed, her finger like an arrow. Did she see the wolf? Or my note from Granny? I looked, but the paper must have blown away because it was nowhere to be seen. "Do you want to explain this, little ghoul?"

Chapter 25

She couldn't know about any of those things. I couldn't tell her. She'd just never understand.

"Not really." Oops. I didn't mean for that to slip out! "I mean, maybe in the morning?" My voice went up on the end changing my statement into a question. Dang it! Why do I always do that when I'm nervous?

"It is morning. Besides, I asked you a question." Mort tapped her foot on the floor and beads of sweat formed on my lip. "Where did you get this clean shirt?"

The shirt? A hot burst of air escaped my lips and I didn't realize I'd been holding my breath. "I . . . uh . . ." I couldn't tell her about Granny. And she wouldn't believe me if I told her it belonged to Cindy. All she'd have to do was call her parents to learn the truth. My brain hurt from trying to think. "I stopped by the store."

"The store. Really?" Mort's eyebrows knit together.

Drac didn't buy my excuse. "It took you all night to buy a shirt at the store?"

"Well . . ." I had to think of something, quick! "I wanted a snack, too. I was starving." I rubbed my belly, bending forward in an overly melodramatic expression, trying to show just how hungry I'd been. "So, I uh . . . just went to the forest . . . for dinner . . ." I studied the old suckers faces to see if they were buying it.

"But we told you—no hunting. It's too dangerous. Why didn't you listen?" Mort's eyes were somewhat sympathetic even if her voice sounded authoritative.

"I know you said hunting was off limits . . . but my stomach was like a big, black, empty hole!" My words were tight in my throat, and I swallowed hard, forcing them down into the pit of my belly to mingle with the cookies and milk. But they didn't get along very well because my stomach rumbled in pain. "I didn't know when we'd eat next and it's hard to be in school all day with all those yummy smelling middle-schoolers."

"That's no excuse." Mort dropped her head a bit. It broke my undead heart to see her so disappointed. "You should know by now we won't let you go hungry."

"Oh and what did you have? Coyote? Perhaps maybe some wolf?" Drac folded his arms across his chest.

I gasped. Did they really know about the wolf? Could they know about Ethan? "Ewh. Gross. You know I hate dogs." Thinking I acted smart, I said, "Beef tartar. Very fresh, too."

"Funny." Mort wasn't amused. "You're telling me you found cattle in the middle of the forest?"

"Yeah. You should . . ." I was about to tell her to try it sometime but realized that if she went into the forest she might find grandmother's house and then I wouldn't be able to visit Granny anymore. "You should just . . . go to your coffin. Like me. Because I'm dead tired." I faked a yawn, stretching my arms overhead.

Dark circles sagged under Mort's eyes. She nodded and yawned. I had her on my side. She understood.

"You're not getting off the hook so easy, little ghoul." Drac's strong military bearing was really a bit overbearing.

"She's just a ghoul and you should be proud that she . . ."

". . . didn't attack a security guard . . ." I chimed in. "You know what happened last time. The military didn't take kindly to all those missing guards."

Drac clicked his heels and marched out of the room.

Mort went after him.

I went to the backdoor and gazed out the window into the forest. The wolf's golden eyes glowed through the thicket of trees and leaves. They seemed softer now. Less scary than before. Maybe because I was in the safety of my warm home.

He raised his muzzle in the air and howled, loud and long. It wasn't terrifying like all the other times. It seemed sad and lonely.

"Night people," I called to the old suckers who were whisper-arguing in Drac's office. "See you later." Without waiting for a response, I hurried off to my room, taking the stairs two at a time.

Once in my room, I collapsed into my coffin—without even brushing my fangs. Parents were so exhausting to deal with. I was ready for some killer beauty rest. Plus, those cookies weren't settling too well and the only remedy for that was a nice, long nap. My eyes closed, heavy with sleep.

It seemed like I'd barely slept when Mort opened my lid. She still looked exhausted. "Want to watch a movie with me?"

I sat up, rubbing my eyes. Sleep sounded better than a movie, but it had been a long time since Mort had asked me to do anything with her. "Sure, I guess." Maybe she didn't hate me. Maybe she sincerely tried to love me, even when I was completely unlovable.

"It's already started. I'm going to get changed and I'll be there in a minute."

I nodded. If Mort tried, so could I. So I washed up quickly and changed into clean clothes—a pair of boot cut jeans (at least they weren't uncomfortable like those skinny ones) and a thin gray sweater. I tossed the white shirt from Granny in my laundry basket and went downstairs.

Moments later Mort came downstairs in her favorite pair of pajamas, her eyes still bloodshot with worry. "It's a pajama day for me," she said. "After the night your father and I had, searching all over for you, I need to settle in and chill out. You probably should, too." She curled up on the couch with a blanket and a bag of her favorite chips.

She handed me the bag. Cheetoes. No, not Cheetos. These are Cheetoes—they're the toes of cheetahs. Occasionally there's a tiger or two. But mostly cheetah. Mort loves them for their crunchy bone marrow flavor. I bet Ethan would love something like that. Dogs love bones. Ugh! Why did I even care about that dog-boy?

For some reason thinking of Ethan and bones reminded me of Cindy. Cindy! I needed to call her. I hadn't seen her since yesterday at the carnival and I probably needed to see if her Dad had recovered. After all, I did make him scream like a girl . . . and pass out cold.

But I didn't know her number. And I didn't know where she lived. So I'd probably just have to wait for school on Monday.

I plopped on the couch next to Mort and grabbed a handful of Cheetoes. The doorbell rang and I jumped up to answer it, the snacks flying out of my hands and spilling all over the floor.

I peeked through the transom window on the door. On the front stoop stood Cindy. That girl must have read my mind! Or maybe I developed amazing super powers that transmitted my thoughts to others.

VAMPIRE RULE #176

Just kidding. Vampires can't magically develop super powers. We're just people. Undead people who feed on blood, but there's nothing magical about that. It's kind of gross if you ask me. Deliciously gross.

Or not.

She held up tickets, pressing them to the window. "Wanna go? It's an afternoon showing."

Nodding, I opened the door, swinging it open wide.

Cindy stepped inside. "I used to go to the midnight showing until . . ." She trailed off mid-sentence, her voice choking up. "Anyway, want to see Star Wars?"

"I don't like war movies. They're too scary for me." They brought back horrible memories.

Cindy laughed. "No, it's not really a war movie. It's a science fiction movie."

"I had enough science in school."

Cindy snorted. "Not that kind of science." She tugged at my arm. "C'mon. Just say yes. It'll be fun."

"Oh, hmmm . . ." I turned toward Mort who was engrossed in her sappy romance movie with sparkling vampires. "Mom . . .?"

"You know, it's so nice to see vampires portrayed in a romantic light," Mort said with a sigh.

I cleared my throat. "Um . . . Mort? We have company."

Mort turned, saw Cindy and leapt up from the couch, dusting Cheetoe crumbs from her pajama top, crunching a few with her feet as she stumbled to the door. "Well," Mort inhaled deeply, lifting her nose in the air as if she were trying to smell Cindy's sweet blood. "What's that?"

"It's Cindy. She took me to the carnival yesterday, remember?"

"Of course I remember," she laughed. "No, I mean, what's that. . ." she sniffed again. ". . . interesting aroma?"

Didn't she remember that I'd told her of Cindy's dirt and autumn leaves fragrance? "Perfume."

"Oh. Right. Your new perfume," Mort said as she tucked a strand of hair behind her ear, smartly covering-up her near goof.

"So, can I go?" Not waiting for her answer, I crossed to the coat rack and grabbed my fedora.

Cindy held up her tickets for Mort to see.

"Star Wars, huh?" Mort gazed into the distance as if remembering a long-forgotten time. "Brings back memories." She licked her lips. Uh-oh. I knew where this memory would take us. Probably not one for visitors to hear. Especially if we were trying to blend in.

"Well, I'm sure we'd love to hear about that another time. Right, Cindy?"

Cindy's eyes widened, looking a bit nervous. "Memories . . ." Cindy sighed softly, her gaze drifting off into the distance.

Mort's face brightened, thinking about her past. "Many years ago I spent a lot of time at the theatre watching this with a dear, dear friend. I hadn't seen her in a long time." Mort's eyes flooded with tears. "I received a funeral announcement a few weeks ago."

My brain suddenly remembered Mort's recent trip. She hadn't told me where she was going or why. It felt like yet another secret she kept hidden. "That's when you went out of town for a few days?" I asked.

Cindy blinked. "My mom and I used to go together every year."

"Is your Mom going tonight?" I reached for the tickets, noticing only two.

"No." Cindy kicked at the ground, her blue converse sneakers making a scuffing sound. "My mom passed away recently."

Mort gasped. "I never noticed the resemblance before..." Mort got wobbly and fell to her knees. She took Cindy's hand and held it tightly between her own. "I see it now ... the hair ... the eyes."

Considering the circumstances it would have been normal for Cindy to jerk away from Mort, but she just stood there. "You..." She blinked. Once. Twice. "You look familiar..."

Mort's lips stretched into a melancholy smile, half-happy, half-undead-heartbroken. "You're Tabitha's girl?"

Cindy stumbled backwards. "You knew my mother?"

Chapter 26

"Wait. You knew her mother?"

Mort tipped her head to the side, as if she were remembering Tabitha fondly. "One of the best witches I ever knew."

"Wait." I was so confused. "But I thought you hated witches."

Mort's eyes hardened, as if she were thinking back to another time, a memory which haunted her. "Some of them aren't to be trusted." She placed her hands on Cindy's shoulders, her eyes twinkling with pride. "But your mother . . . Tabitha . . . well, she was one of the great ones."

"I miss her," Cindy said, her voice quivering.

"Me too." Mort wiped away her tears. "Now, you best be going before you're late for the show."

When we arrived, Sarah waited near the ticket booth, holding three boxes of candy. "I got your favorite." She handed chocolate Whoppers to Cindy. "But I didn't know what you liked, Scarlet, so I hope this is okay."

I took the box of Hot Tamales. "This is perfect. Thanks." It was nice of her to think of me.

The smell of werewolf let me know Ethan was here too. Sure enough, he and his brother stepped out from behind a sign, each holding a large tub of popcorn and a fountain soda. When they saw me, they didn't say anything. But there were plenty of words in their unblinking stares. Kind of like my parent's whisper-conversations.

We filed into our seats in the theatre. Cindy, then Ethan, followed by Sarah and Hunter. I shuffled in last, sitting next to Hunter, who'd never spoken a word to me. I assumed that, like his brother, he didn't like me much. Between Ethan's wolfy odor and Cindy's earthy smell, my nose was picking up something rank.

"What's that smell?" I asked, grabbing my fedora and placing it over my nose to block out the odor. This was a little more pungent than typical Ethan wolf-stink.

Dirty looks glared from all directions; Cindy with her jaw open, Ethan with a scowl, and Sarah whose eyebrows knit together quizzically. But the worse one of all—Hunter, who glared lividly, pinching his lips into a thin, angry line. His amber eyes made me uneasy. Maybe the smell wasn't Ethan. Maybe it was Hunter . . .

"I . . . I forgot to wash my feet." Ethan leaned across both

Sarah and Hunter, red flooding his face. "Could you please shut up—just once—about my smell?"

"Maybe you should go urinate on a fire hydrant. Or chew a bone." I balled my hand into a fist, but when I saw everyone watching me, I made myself relax. I was probably over reacting to the whole thing anyway. I wasn't used to friends and I really wasn't sure about the whole werewolf thing either, even if he did know my secret and helped me out of a very sticky cherry-pie, vampire-fang situation.

"Uh, I mean . . ." I muttered, not able to think of anything to say. I couldn't recover from the comment I'd just made. Boys were jerks. Especially wolf-boys like Ethan. But sometimes vampire girls were pretty dumb, too.

"What's eating you?" Ethan said between handfuls of popcorn.

Hunter laughed. "You mean, what did she eat?"

"What's that supposed to mean?" I clenched my fist again and a handful of popcorn crumbled to the floor. Ethan already knew my vampire status, but I thought he'd kept my secret. Maybe I was wrong and he'd told Hunter. What if Ethan knew about my trip to Granny's house? Would he keep that information quiet, too? Ugh! If he didn't, I'd have no choice but to take him down.

Sarah chimed in. "You know, the cherry pie mess. It must have given you a stomach ache."

I unclenched my hands. "Oh right, that." Still, I couldn't help but wonder if Ethan had spilled the beans. I didn't know what I'd do if he ratted me out. "Yeah. Haha. Funny."

"So after the show," Cindy started, changing the subject, "we're all going to the diner for something to eat."

"Tradition," Sarah finished matter-of-factly.

I shrugged, calming down. "Sure, I'm in."

Music blasted into the theatre and images flickered on the screen.

"Sshhh, it's starting," Ethan said, stating the obvious.

Even though I liked movies, I would never understand this one. Flying aircraft, a giant hairy dog that walked upright (which I'm sure Ethan loved), lots of guns with brightly colored bullets and glowing swords that made strange noises ... it was just a bunch of nonsense. But it made my friends happy, so I acted like I enjoyed it too.

When the credits rolled, I placed my fedora back on my head so low and tight it nearly hid my eyes.

We traveled a few blocks to Jack Sprats House of Fats.

Everyone ordered milkshakes. Cindy got the funny bones shake, a combination of chocolate and peanut butter. Her obsession with bones baffled me. Sarah ordered the grasshopper, which resembled the green bug because of its color, but really it was just crème de menthe with chocolate chips. The girls shared a vegetarian burger with a double order of fries. What was it with humans and their fries?

Wolf-boy and Hunter both ordered vanilla milkshakes and triple decker bison burgers with extra bacon and opted for a side of pickled pigs' feet instead of coleslaw. Figures. Werewolves like Ethan loved their meat, even when they were in human form. He probably even wanted to eat the squirrel I'd caught in the woods. They also ordered a platter of onion rings with Jack Sprat's special sauce which was nothing more than a mayonnaise concoction with herbs and spices.

Me? I couldn't order a Bloody Tom or people might know my secret, so I got the next best thing: vegetable juice. Straight up. With a stalk of celery. They didn't have cheetoes or passion fruit on the menu. Heck, they didn't even have necktarines or blood oranges!

"Vegetable juice?" Sarah wrinkled her nose in disgust.

Cindy curled her skinny arms, making a muscle. "Did you have your V8 today?"

I sunk in my seat, lowering my fedora until it hid my mouth from view. If I got too excited my fangs might just pop out again.

Ethan laughed so hard, vanilla milkshake spurted out of his nose. It reminded me of snot.

I put my hat back on my head, and stuck my chin out, pretending to be upset. "Mock me all you like, but it's delicious." Lifting the drink to my lips, I took a gulp. "Ah. Tasty." I dabbed the corners of my mouth with a napkin trying to act sophisticated.

What followed would soon become known as the Food Fight Fantastical.

Ethan crammed a pickled pig's foot in his mouth. He reached across the table and shoved one at Cindy. Cindy wasn't too fond of this. I rather enjoy a pig's foot every now and again, but Cindy flung it back at him. Ethan ducked and it smacked a diner behind him in the back of the head.

The older gentleman turned around and yelled. "Hey you brat kids! Watch what you're doing!" He had a head large enough to be a pumpkin. Even if he hadn't yelled, I wouldn't have thought he was the nicest man around. He just had a cranky expression on his face, a warning that he'd steal my bike or crush my scooter if he found it in his yard.

"Sorry, Mr. Peterkin," Cindy said, sinking in to her seat.

Mr. Peterkin resumed eating his meal with a very loud humpf.

Sarah shoved a fistful of fries into her mouth and mimicked the cranky man, making a face at him. But when she tried to talk it just came across as a mumble. Hunter didn't seem happy about any of it and he reached for the tray of onion rings, knocking over his milkshake in the process. Most of the mess landed in Ethan's lap and he leapt up, with a yelp. The table nearly toppled and the remaining drinks spilled, splattering onto Cindy's top. She gasped.

I hid behind my fedora again, blindly throwing a handful of mushy, wet food. I peeked out from behind my hat to see a waitress standing there, tapping her foot.

"Uh-hmmm." She cleared her throat, placing the check on the table with a nasty glare. We probably hadn't been the nicest—or neatest—customers.

On the way home my friends chatted the whole time while I struggled to stay awake through all the boring girl

talk. It had once been interesting and fun in my younger years. But now it had become kind of mind-numbing since I'd heard it all. But I tried to act interested because I supposed that's what friends do. One by one my friends filed off to their houses, Ethan and Hunter first, followed by Sarah, until only Cindy remained.

"I'll walk you the rest of the way," Cindy offered. "You know, so you don't have to go alone."

"But then you'll be by yourself."

"Oh, I don't mind," she quickly responded. Somehow I had a feeling she was up to something.

The sun began to sink in the horizon while my thoughts drifted to Granny. I missed her, the yummy cookies, and her sweet grandma-ness. After all, I really didn't want to go home and be with my gloomy family after the almost-best-day-of-my-life.

"Really. I'm okay. You go ahead. I'll be fine for the last few blocks on my own."

"Well, if you're sure . . ." Cindy let out a sigh as she nervously glanced around. If I didn't know any better, I'd swear she seemed slightly relieved.

I nodded. "Thanks for the fun afternoon."

"See you tomorrow." She took off before I could say anything more. Running like a skinny skeleton of a girl.

As soon as she was out of sight, I darted toward the woods.

Chapter 27

Dusk gave everything an eerie orange haze, and as I approached the Parkview Cemetery, the strangest sight appeared before my eyes. A skeleton danced in front of the gates, petting a wolf. Actually, it was a werewolf. If I were a betting girl, I'd say it was Ethan. I took a deep breath. The smell of his dogginess punched my nostrils, making me want to keel over.

The skeleton climbed over the gate, and with a nudge from wolf-boy, ran toward the back of the cemetery. The bones clinked and clanked until they vanished from sight.

I rubbed my eyes, unable to believe what I'd just seen. "What was that?"

The werewolf perked his ears.

Oh no! He'd heard me. If I slipped into the shadows, he might not see me. I tiptoed back one step. Then another.

My foot slipped on a rock and I tripped, falling with a loud "Humpf!"

The werewolf jerked his head. His green eyes reflected the glow of the street lights as he approached stealthily, one step at a time, like a dog sneaking up behind its owner, ready to nip his ankles. In one blink, he bared his teeth, saliva dripping from his jowls.

Mort was right about werewolves. They were moody and unpredictable. Maybe Ethan would be nice since we'd just had a fun time together.

No such luck. The wolf charged, his feet pounding on the pavement, as he ran straight toward me.

Run, Scarlet, RUNNNN!

I ran. Fast. Thank goodness my feet and brain cooperated, because I made a sharp turn to the left just as the wolf's hot breath swept down my back.

Darting between two trees, my fedora blew off. "No!" I yelped, as I turned to see it float away into the night. My favorite fedora of all time. Clyde gave it to me. Yes, the infamous Clyde of Bonnie and Clyde, the fangsters. Sure, it was a little beat up after all these years, but that's what made it so special.

Desperate, I changed directions, chasing after the hat. But that stupid wolf was close, and if he had his way, I'd be his next meal. I stretched out my arm, determined to get my hat back, but my fedora lifted into the air with the breeze and drifted away, like a surfboard on a wave.

I watched desperately, as the hat bounced around, finally it landing on a tree branch, several feet in the air.

Jumping up, I swiped at the branch, hoping that it would release my fedora. I leapt up again, the werewolf growling behind me. I landed (without my hat), and turned around slowly, so as to not upset him.

"Nice doggie," I said in the calmest voice ever. Like that would work. I'd seen how well that helped in the past. "Just let me get my hat . . ." maybe persuasion was the way to get moody wolves to cooperate. ". . . and I'll be on my merry way, and you can be on yours."

A deep noise rumbled from deep in Ethan's gut. He snarled and snapped at the air.

Desperate, I jumped up one last time and swiped at the branch. The fedora escaped the branches, tumbling all the way down. The wolf leapt into the air, chomping the hat into his mouth.

Ethan was supposed to be my friend. Why was he taking something I cared so deeply about? "Drop it," I demanded, gesturing with a pointed finger. This giant-excuse-for-a-dog might be a werewolf, but he wasn't going to take my fedora. "I said—'Drop it!' That's my hat."

The wolf shook his head furiously. Fur, slobber and my hat flew through the air, landing between us.

My hat! Dog-boy dropped it! It was only inches away. I felt brave—or stupid—and inched closer. If I could just get my hat back . . .

Ethan growled low and deep, his eyes turning into angry

slits of green. He licked his chops, drool dripping from his jowls. Ethan snapped at the air, a gust of warm air blowing across my skin as he barely missed my hand with his fierce teeth.

Tears welled up. He could have killed me with one bite. "Fine. Keep it. Stupid dog." I backed away.

The wolf stalked forward, his vicious teeth making me quiver. I didn't want to be dog food. I stepped back into a tree, cornered. "Don't bite me," I whispered, my body shaking with fear.

Ethan plopped down on the ground, picked up my precious fedora and began ripping it to pieces. If his mouth was busy with my hat, at least that meant he couldn't bite me. I'd miss my favorite fedora as Fido tore it to shreds . . . but at least he wouldn't be doing it to me, and I could escape.

I took off running, heading toward the forest, straight for Granny's house, like I wanted to in the first place. I glanced back once and watched the wolf gnawing at my hat as if it were a bone.

Branches snapped, thorns clawed at my clothes. I burst through the trees, breathless and panting, onto the neatly groomed lawn. I made it to Granny's house, safe and sound. The werewolf was nowhere to be seen. Or heard. Thank Hades.

"Well, dearie, I thought you'd never arrive." Granny's needles clinked against each other as she knitted furiously. When she put her needles down on the bench, the spool of yarn rolled to my feet.

Still panting, I reached to retrieve it for her, but she shouted out, "I've got that!" Granny inched her way off the bench, accompanied by great grunts and groans. Being old was for the birds. I think it was one of the first times I was grateful to have my young vampire body.

"Okay," I said. My lips were dry and they stuck to my teeth in an awkward, painful grin.

"Looks like you could use a drink," she said once she'd retrieved her ball of yarn and hobbled to the door. Granny waved her hand inside, the glow of a warm fire lighting the entrance. "How about a nice, cool glass of ice water?"

That sounded more pleasant than it usually did. "I'd like . . . that . . ." I said between pants and gulps of air. ". . . very . . . much."

Granny led me inside to the same room I'd been in during my previous visit. While she waddled off into the kitchen I sat on the sofa near the fireplace. The cozy, warm room made me so sleepy. Sparks shot from the fireplace, dancing onto the floor. They slowed, swirling in a display of red and gold until I felt dizzy and the room spun like a Ferris wheel. I hoped Granny would return with the drink before I fell into a nice little slumber. My eyelids were so heavy, like lead weights.

Woods flashed. Trees. Bushes. Brush. Stinging, scratching branches. I ran and ran. I'd never felt so exhausted in all my vampire life. But I couldn't stop. Something chased me. Something evil and dark. Something that lurked in the woods with glowing yellow eyes. Putrid eyes, filled with evil.

"Wake up, dearie," Granny called.

I opened my eyes to see a tray of drinks and muffins on the coffee table.

Before Granny could even offer me the drink of water, I guzzled it down, slamming my glass on the table when I was done.

"Well . . ." Granny surveyed my empty cup. ". . . would you like a refill?"

"No thanks." I grabbed a muffin, taking a generous bite. I wanted to scarf down everything in sight. "These are . . ." Crumbs flew from my mouth as I spoke. ". . . the best muffins I've ever had."

"I'm glad you like them."

"Aren't you going to have one?" I lifted the plate and shoved it at her.

"Oh, no, dearie. Granny never eats sweets."

"More for me," I said grabbing the second muffin. "What kind of muffins are these anyway?"

"Chocolate surprise. They're my spec-i-al-i-ty," Granny said with a wink.

"What's that . . . unique flavor?" I savored the morsels in my mouth. There was a detectable chocolate flavor, but something else . . . something familiar, yet . . . I couldn't quite put my finger on it.

"Oh, Granny never tells, dearie." She leaned back in her chair, the cushions sinking beneath her.

"Well, they're the best I've ever tasted." I reached for

the other glass of water, but stopped when I realized I was probably being rude.

"Go ahead, dearie. It's all yours."

I gulped the water, rinsing down the remains of the chocolate muffin.

Granny coughed and pulled a blanket onto her lap.

"Maybe I should bring you a treat the next time I visit."

Granny huffed on her glasses. "That's not necessary." She polished the lenses with the edge of her blouse. "Besides, your visits with me are to escape the world. The demands of your parents. You need someone to understand you, don't you?"

I nodded.

"Granny is here for you." She inched out of her seat. "Now, how about another muffin?"

My stomach had a satisfied ache in it to the point where I worried it might explode. "No, thank you." I patted my belly like a toddler. "I'm pretty full."

"Wonderful!" Granny threw her head back and cackled.

Maybe an old lady cackling like a witch would make most people uncomfortable, but since I was a vampire, stuff like that didn't really bother me. Even if Mort never liked witches and she'd warned about them, I felt like I could trust Granny. Especially since now I knew there were nice witches, like Cindy's mom.

Granny waddled off into the kitchen and I followed close behind, settling into a dining chair. "Would you like to stay for dinner?" She turned, holding a butcher knife, its silver blade reflecting the flickering flames of the fire. Granny cackled and cawed, her face distorted in the lighting. The knife glistened as she drew it back and grinned.

Chapter 28

She slammed the knife into a head of purple cabbage, the vegetable splitting in two, divided perfectly down the center. "I make a mean cabbage stew." She chopped until each piece became a perfect, bite-sized morsel.

I don't know when my fingers had dug into the arm of the chair, but my grip loosened as I breathed deep. Noticing the late hour, dusk teasing the horizon, I realized I hadn't been home in hours and the old suckers were probably worried. Again. They probably had the police out on a missing person's search. Which meant I'd be grounded for good this time.

"You're not worried about your parents, are you?" Granny pulled a package of stew meat from the fridge, dumping it into the pot. It sizzled as it hit the hot oil. The room filled with a wonderful, comforting aroma.

My mouth watered as my eyes fell upon the blood-stained package.

VAMPIRE RULE #180

Don't drool when you see things only vampires have appetites for. You'll look weird, even to the most understanding of people.

"Would you . . ." Granny grinned sheepishly. "Would you like the drippings?"

I couldn't control it a moment longer. I hadn't had a fresh kill in so long it surprised me that I hadn't attacked the entire town. And although Granny's sweets had satisfied me in a way only a fresh-kill could, I still longed for one yummy lick of those drippings. Grabbing the package from Granny, I shoved it in my face so she couldn't see my fangs. It wasn't like I needed them anyway, but still. Within seconds I'd licked the package clean.

Talk about awkward. I might have just as well said, "Hey Granny, by the way, I'm a vampire." That would have gone over well. Not.

"Well, that changes things a bit, now doesn't it?" Granny groaned in an odd sort of way.

I wiped the sleeve of my shirt across my mouth. "Anemic." I said with a nod. "Forgot to take my pills this morning." Obviously I lied, but maybe Granny would fall for it.

"Of course. Of course. Anemics need lots of iron-rich foods."

"Yes, that's it."

"Well, next time you visit I'll make sure I have something very special for you."

My mind swirled with the possibilities. Raccoon. Beaver. Deer. Sheep. Man, I could even go for a cougar. I was too tired for that kind of fight, though normally it really got me pumping with excitement.

"Why don't you tell me about your parents, dearie?"

Cat. Ferret. Dog. I shook my head. Was I crazy? I hated dog. "What, what was that?"

"Your parents, dearie?" Granny said again, slicing her blade through a red beet. Juice seeped out, staining her wooden cutting board a shade of purple.

"My parents?" I scratched at my arm. "You know, they're parents."

"Of course. Miserable folk. Never understand anything."

She must have had parents at one point, so she had to know what that was like. "Dad's in the military. We move a lot. Usually because I get into trouble."

Granny sliced another beet, her eyes steady on her work. "Ah . . . I see."

"I'm not bad or anything."

"Of course not, dearie. Parents just don't understand, do they?"

"Not at all," I grumped. "Mort's like a thousand years old."

"She's old fashioned, eh?"

"No, she's quite literally . . ." I caught myself. ". . . quite old fashioned."

"She wants to protect you, keep you safe, but you want to be free to grow up and make your own decisions. Even your own mistakes."

My eyes snapped up. "Exactly!"

"Well," she stirred the contents of the pot, "maybe you should just make your mistakes."

"Maybe I should!" Granny gave me the courage I needed to be bold, brave, and capable. I didn't need my parents. I didn't need friends. I didn't need anyone.

Wait.

That didn't sound like me. That didn't feel like me either! I would always need the old suckers. Maybe just not in the way I was used to. I liked having friends, too. Especially since I'd just made them for the first time in a really long time. "On second thought . . ."

Granny peered over the top of her glasses. She held up a spoon filled with stew. "Taste."

I gulped it down. "Delicious!" I exclaimed. "Like lamb stew." My favorite.

"Well, I succeeded." Granny's grin stretched from ear to ear. "Have a seat." She gestured to a square table situated in the corner.

We each took a seat at the little square table, a bowl of stew for both of us. An ivory topcoat had brush strokes and large globs of hardened paint. Pieces of it were chipped off, mostly around the edges. Beneath that a rainbow of colors struggled to be seen. Granny must have painted that table a hundred times!

I put my hand on the table and it seemed to squirm. I jerked my hand away. Granny groaned, and the table stilled.

After two mega-sized muffins and a couple large glasses of water (not to mention the blood drippings from the meat package), I really shouldn't have been hungry. Something about Granny's cooking begged me to eat more. So I shoveled heaping spoonfuls of stew into my mouth. When I finished, I wiped my mouth, letting out a humongous belch.

"I've never been—"

"Sorry," I interrupted, my cheeks growing hot with embarrassment.

"—so impressed in all my life!" Granny patted my back as if she were burping a baby. "I'm glad you enjoyed it."

"Thank you, Granny. You're so nice. And kind. And you make the best food ever. And you understand me." It all came blurting out and there was no controlling the words that spewed from my mouth.

"I'm glad you feel that way." Granny stood with a grunt. She toddled across the room tending to a whistling kettle. "Now, how about a nice, hot cup of tea?"

I felt like my belly would pop. "No thank you, Granny. If I have one more thing I might just explode."

"Ah, but this tea will help settle all that food." Granny handed me the steaming cup of tea.

"Well, all right. If you say so." I sipped at the tea, warm chamomile and cinnamon, reminding me of my childhood days. My eyes became heavy with memories and I sunk into my chair. My body twirled and floated around the room.

Was I dreaming? This was all in my imagination. Surely it was nothing more. Or was it?

A vision of green eyes appeared in the darkness. "Scarlet," the eyes seemed to whisper to my mind. "You must go now. It isn't safe here."

"But I like Granny's house," my mind whispered back. I'm pretty sure I never actually spoke the words. They were just thoughts in my head. "She helps me. I feel safe." My mind begged the glowing eyes to understand. All I ever wanted was to be understood. Accepted.

"Granny isn't who she says she is." Those comforting green eyes burrowed their message into my mind.

"But I don't want to leave." My crusty heart ached a little. The thought of leaving Granny and going back to a home where I was misunderstood made me feel miserable inside. No one trusted me except Granny. If that's all who would ever trust me—and if that's the only person I could trust—it was better than nothing and I wouldn't let anyone take that away.

"Go now!" the voice snapped suddenly. A low rumble echoed in my head. It grew into a massive roar. A mouth full of fangs, white and bright as the moon, shot through the darkness.

Chapter 29

My eyelids burst open.

"You all right, dearie?" Granny's pearly whites glowed softly. She picked up the knitting in her lap and held it to the ceiling, studying her handiwork. "Bad dream?"

The image of fangs and warnings haunted me. "Uh, yeah. Bad dream." My unfeeling heart beat in my chest, making me so nervous and jittery my hands trembled.

"How about another nice cup of tea?" Granny knit, her hands making loops, the needles tapping and tinkling against each other as she worked.

My head throbbed. My stomach ached. "No!" I shouted.

Granny's eyes narrowed.

VAMPIRE RULE #184

Don't be rude to little old ladies. Especially when they feed you goodies and treats. They might not be so nice in the future and you've got to take all the kindness you can get when you're a middle-school vampire.

Realizing my tone, I quickly corrected. "I mean, no thank you, Granny."

Her voice sharpened. "How about a cookie?"

Sometimes my vampire instincts were slow, but I started to feel as though I should go home. The faster the better. "Uh, no thank you."

As if she read my mind, Granny said, "You best be on your way now." Did she look angry?

I rubbed my eyes. No. She couldn't be angry. Granny was a real sweetheart.

A grin stretched across her face as pleasant as Mrs. Claus. "Don't forget your hat." Granny seemed to pull a fedora from thin air.

My heart leapt in my chest. My fedora! "But . . . how did you find that? I lost it when the—"

"The wolf chased you." A little wad of spittle gathered in the corner of Granny's mouth. "I know, dearie. I know. Granny always knows."

I started to think she was like Mrs. Claus. Better yet, Santa himself!

"I have something else for you." Granny excused herself from the room. She returned a moment later with a beautiful red cape. "This'll keep you safe from those nasty wolves. They don't like red much. Must remind them of bloodshed. "

That made me shiver because red reminded me of

bloodshed, too, which usually made me hungry. But this time it just made me feel sick.

Granny draped the crimson cape over my shoulders, pulling the hood up and over my head. The silky fabric cascaded around me, in a lovely swirl of color. Granny admired the cloak. "A scarlet cape for my dear Scarlet. Fitting, don't you think?"

"I love it." I gave my new cape a twirl. It swirled around me like giant wings. It reminded me of Shade, and I wondered where he went. If I'd ever see him again.

Granny took my fedora and placed it on my head.

It was a tad awkward wearing a hooded cape and a hat, but I wasn't about to insult Granny and her kindness. She was just about the nicest person I'd ever met and my parents always told me to respect my elders.

A midnight sky hugged the house, darkness painting the windows. Time seemed to go faster when I was with Granny. "Well, I guess I better be on my way."

Granny nodded, her gray curls bouncing like tiny springs.

"Thanks for everything, Granny." I spun one last time, showing off my beautiful cape. "See you tomorrow."

"You know I wouldn't miss it for the world." Granny wiped spittle from the corner of her mouth before waving goodbye.

"Great. See you then." The slam of the door made my stomach do a little flip.

Outside, the sky changed from black midnight to cat's-eye gold.

VAMPIRE RULE #186

Pay attention to clues. It might just save your afterlife.

Leaves rustled in the breeze, like millions of bugs crawling on the ground. Animals scurried, made screeching noises, and eyes watched me.

Despite the goose bumps that rose on my arms, covering my skin like an infectious disease, I kept pressing forward despite the ominous gold sky (which, if my life were a movie, would have been accompanied by ominous music). You'd think I'd be scared. But I wasn't. Goose bumps don't always mean fear. I was cold. That's all.

VAMPIRE RULE #80

Wear warmer clothes. Just because you're a vampire doesn't mean you can't get cold.

So I pulled my cape closer, until I looked like a red hotdog, the kind that are spicy and set your taste buds on fire. Or perhaps a Zagnut—a red wrapper securing a sweet and sugary candy, though maybe a little nutty on the inside. I guess whichever you choose because both are tasty, if you ask me.

The forest closed in as I realized I didn't want to look like someone's snack.

It was so hard to breathe, it felt like someone had swaddled me tight in cloth. Oh, wait. I was sort of swaddled. The bright red beautiful cape Granny had given me was wrapped around my body like a glove. No wonder I felt like I was suffocating! I loosened the cape and let it fall freely at my side. Not that loosening the cape helped my fear.

More noises echoed in the forest and a lump stuck in my throat. Tree branches stretched across the path, like gnarled witches hands reaching out to grab me and drag me into their clutches. Or their black cauldron. And turn me into soup. Or maybe a potion for everlasting life.

I gulped. That couldn't happen to me! I needed to live my afterlife!

Calm down, Scarlet.

Besides, even if you were to boil me up, and mix me with enchantments, you couldn't pass on the curse of eternal life without the bite from a vampire. And everyone knows if you get bit by a vampire you're either a tasty meal or you become a vampire too. It's vampire rule number one. Don't you remember it? Everyone knows it. Look it up.

There's always a price to pay for eternal life, anyway.

My price? Repeating middle school, forever and ever and ever. I'll never have a chance to change or grow old. As ugly as growing old is, it certainly has its perks.

One: Driving a car. Nope. Never gonna happen.

The wind howled, blowing my cape behind me. I pulled my hood tight under my chin.

Two: Going on a date. Yeah, dating thirteen year-old boys when you're over one hundred isn't quite the same thing.

Trees creaked. My knees knocked with each step.

Three: No homework. Well, sure, you'll have to do it during college—but college is only a few years, it doesn't go until you're forty . . . unless you're Drac. Even though he's in the military he always finds an excuse to go back to school. You'll be a perpetual student, going to school forever and ever. And he's like centuries old and he hasn't stopped yet. UGH!

A branch crashed behind me, and I lost my footing, falling into a pile of leaves. Focus, Scarlet. Don't be scared.

Four: Not being hounded by your parents. But I've heard that one doesn't change a whole lot. Weird.

The eerie sky glowed behind me, lighting Granny's house. Was it my imagination or did it seem different than it had before?

Five: Holding a job. Okay, that one's not so great because you're only hounded by a boss.

Six: Creaky knees, achy joints, gray hair, and false teeth. Hmmmm . . . staying young forever didn't look so bad after all.

A crash echoed through the forest, like a tree falling to the ground. If there was something large enough to take down a tree, it was certainly big enough to take care of a little vampire.

The hairs on my arms stood on end. I had to get out of the forest. Why was it taking so long to get home? Was I lost? Why couldn't I ever find my way?

The wind whipped my face, as I pressed forward, struggling with every step. Another gust swept my fedora into the air. It hovered a moment before the wind sent it spiraling. I leapt after it, but it tumbled through the forest, straight into a pile of rocks at the base of a large tree. Stumbling onto the mound, I reached for my hat. Inches from it, my fingers almost touching the worn fabric, a hand shot out from the mound, grabbing my wrist.

Chapter 30

Terrified, I jerked away. The hand snapped and I tumbled backward, smacking my head on the ground. I sat up, rubbing the sore spot. A part of the hand held on to the rim of my fedora. Wrapping my fingers around it, I pried it free. But the hand felt funny. Something wasn't right.

It wasn't a hand at all. "A tree branch?" I panted. "I was afraid of a stupid branch?"

I exhaled shakily. I needed to get home before my imagination got the better of me.

A break in the trees revealed a beautiful rainbow hue of sunrise. Beyond the last few trees I saw the green grass of my backyard. Home! Home at last.

I trudged up the back steps and held my breath as I tried the handle. To my surprise, the handle turned easily in my grasp. I snuck inside to a darkened house. The old suckers were asleep. At first, I felt disappointed. After the trek I'd just suffered through the woods, nothing sounded better than one of Mort's hugs. But as least if they were asleep, they couldn't be angry.

I hunkered down on the couch, a Bloody Tom on the table, Cheetoes at my side, and a book in my lap. My beautiful cape wrapped around me like a blanket. There was nothing suspicious about this. At all.

After a few bites, my stomach felt funny. Even though there were only a few hours before school and I hadn't slept in ages, I decided to listen to my die pod. As soon as I put in my earbuds, I heard voices in the distance and took them out again. Lots of murmuring and whispering. Familiar voices.

"... not sure anymore ..."

"... safety ... compromised ..."

"... Scarlet ..."

"... fault. .."

"... no choice ..."

Mort? Drac?

I thought they were sleeping. Not only were they awake, but they were talking about me. That was always a bad thing. Plus, from the sounds of it, they still thought my little display at the school carnival had risked our safety.

What was new? Everything was my fault.

Unless they knew I'd been sneaking out. What if they found out about Ethan? Or Granny?

The door handle rattled. I nearly jumped out of my skin when the knob started shaking. They hadn't been in their coffins after all. They were out. Probably hunting.

Keys jingled. They clinked in the keyhole.

I groped at the red cape wrapped around me. I had to think of something fast. If Mort and Drac were still upset about the pie-eating contest, they wouldn't be thrilled to see me wearing a cape from a stranger. I'd never be able to explain Granny.

Think Scarlet, think!

". . . nothing but trouble . . ." The door creaked open.

A figure stepped inside, casting a shadow on the wall. Probably Mort since the silhouette had long hair and a small nose. ". . . got to do something . . ."

Oh no! It was too late to leave the room. They would see me if I ran off. There were only two choices: pretend I was asleep or confront them.

I really wanted to choose the first option. It had always worked before. Usually I could get lots more information, too, because they'd just keep on talking while I fake-snored away. But I was older now, and Mort and Drac were probably on to my tactics. After all, Drac wasn't in the military all this time for nothing.

My gut wrenching, I sat up.

Mort raised an eyebrow as she removed her clip-on earrings. She never liked piercings. Said they hurt too much.

VAMPIRE RULE #72

Whoever said vampires don't feel pain was obviously never a vampire. Just because we're undead doesn't mean we're unalive. Duh.

"What are you reading, Scarlet?"

I held up the book, realizing too late that it was upside down and backwards. "The Vampire's Guide to the Galaxy."

"A classic." Drac said from across the room. "Good ghoul."

Neither of them mentioned the book's position or that I obviously hadn't read a single page. In fact, they were acting suspiciously unsuspicious.

"Scarlet," Mort started. "When . . ."

"Did you get home?" Drac asked.

Mort threw off her coat, missing the rack in the process. Her full skirt swayed as she bustled over.

They seemed worried, not angry, so that was a good thing, right? I knew the casualness was all for show.

"Scarlet Small," Mort started. She crossed her arms and tapped her kitten heels a million-miles-a-minute on the wood floor. So much for not being angry.

I guess I should have been happy she actually cared, but this body language was all too familiar and I knew I was in trouble. My hands trembled. I wrenched them, hard. They still shook. So I shoved them deep in my pockets. "Yes, Mort?"

The last time she started a conversation with Scarlet Small we ended up moving halfway across the world.

"Are you okay?"

I nodded. What a strange question. Why wouldn't I be? Mort rushed over to me. In the dark, her bright red lipstick stood out like crimson rose buds. Even at this hour, her polished skin and perfectly coiffed hair looked like she'd come straight out of a 1950 issue of Good Housekeeping. Mort threw her arms around me, nearly choking me with a hug.

"I'm fine." I coughed. "Really. Perfectly undead."

Mort sighed in relief. "We thought the wolf got you." She broke down into a fit of sobs.

"Wolf?" I gasped so hard my throat burned. They knew about the wolf? How much did they know? Why hadn't they ever let on until now? "I don't know anything about a wolf." My voice waivered with the lie. Remaining calm felt impossible, so I forced my jitters away by biting my lip.

"You haven't smelled him?" Drac's chin dropped. The light from the streetlamps flooded in through the front window making his slicked back hair shine like he'd used too much Brylcreem.

"No." I shook my head. "I haven't smelled a thing." How could I not? But I wasn't about to tell them that. There was no telling what would happen if I confessed that I knew all along.

If they were this upset, what would they do if they knew I'd talked to him? I certainly couldn't tell them about our confrontations in the woods. Or the time he saved my vampire-butt at the carnival. If it hadn't been for his quick-thinking with the fake fangs, the whole town would've known my family's vampire-secret.

"I knew there was trouble the first day. That school reeked with wolf." Mort wiped away her tears, then massaged her temples with her fingertips. That was her stress-headache signal.

So that's why Mort had acted strange! She wasn't upset with me. She was scared of the wolf.

"There's no choice," Drac said in his firm authoritative military voice. "We can't live in a town with a wolf. We have to move."

"No!" I leapt up from the couch faster than a gazelle running from a lion.

The old suckers watched with wide eyes.

"I have a confession to make . . ."

"What is it, Scarlet?" Mort said, her expression difficult to read. She seemed calmer now, not so stressed about the whole wolf thing, especially now that I was home safe and sound.

"I've been visiting . . ." I gulped. I didn't want to confess it. I didn't want anyone to take Granny away from me. "Granny. Well, not my Granny. Just a nice Granny who bakes cookies."

Mort's face flushed a shade of green. "A grandmother you say?"

Drac dropped his hands at his side. "Where does she live?"

"In the woods." I picked at a scab on my arm. I couldn't

believe I told them about Granny all just to protect a stupid wolf-boy! What was wrong with me?

Without a word, the old suckers stalked into Drac's office and had a whisper-conversation. A moment later Mort returned.

"Your father and I just discussed it . . ."

Drac entered the room as if on cue. ". . . that you shouldn't spend so much time with this grandmother of yours. You're breaking the rules, and the woods are dangerous with a wolf on the loose. This has all become a very bad habit. Bad habits must be broken." Drac looked down his nose at me. "Immediately."

"That's not fair!" I stomped my feet like a tantrum-throwing toddler. At least the Granny confession took their minds off the wolf. "But . . . why can't I see her?"

VAMPIRE RULE #56
When you're in already in a heap of trouble, don't sass the old suckers.

On a normal day I would have been scolded for back-talking, but nothing about this would ever be normal. In fact, I began to wonder if there would ever be another normal day again.

"We just think it would be healthier for you to spend time with kids your own age," Mort said, stepping closer, trying to smooth things over.

"But she is my age!" I countered. I mean, really, she was.

I might look like a middle-schooler but I'm as old as any other grandmother—just like Granny. Heck, I'm probably a lot older than her!

Mort almost chuckled. Almost. "She has a point," she said, tipping her head toward Drac.

"Well, none of this is normal." Drac straightened his back. It was his defensive stance. "We have no choice. We have to move."

Dang! They were back to the threat of moving. "NO!" I yelled. "I mean . . . not yet," I said trying to maintain my composure. I just started making friends. Cindy was the closest thing I'd ever had to a best friend. Not to mention, Granny made me feel so special with cookies and gifts. But those reasons wouldn't be enough for my parents. I had to give them something else. Something more.

"I saw a skeleton!"

Chapter 31

"**Y**ou're kidding, right?" Mort placed a hand over her mouth. I couldn't tell if it was disbelief, nausea, or both.

"No, and the wolf was there, too." Oh no! What did I just say? I'd confirmed their worst fear—that I'd seen the wolf.

"The wolf?" Mort stumbled backward. "You've seen him?"

"But don't worry, it's cool. He didn't try to hurt me." It was a lie. He'd stabbed me with a fork, nearly bit my nose off in the woods and chased me every chance he got. But he'd also helped hide my secret.

Mort wobbled on her heels, like she'd pass out.

"There's only one thing to do at a time like this." Drac folded his hands together behind his back and strode up to Mort.

She took the queue, gulping hard. But she recovered

quickly and opened the fridge door. "In the mood for a snack?"

What? How would a snack solve any of this? "No," I said hesitantly, raising my drink. "I'm good."

"No, I mean a real snack."

Translation: sucking the life from a pig, squirrel, cat, dog or some other animal. In other words, vampire food. My stomach churned at the thought. If I could have lost any more coloring in my face I would have, but being a vampire and all, I was pretty pale to begin with.

Mort held up a frozen guinea pig. "You feeling all right, Scarlet?"

Everything in my stomach revolted. It was the Jets against the Sharks. The French Revolution. World War II. And I didn't have the white flag of surrender anywhere. Instead, I had a trashcan.

"Oh, no!" Drac rushed to my side. "Must have been something you ate."

You could say that . . .

"Or didn't eat." Mort handed me the animal. "You haven't had anything healthy in days."

It was true. "I'm fine," I lied.

"It's those wolves," Drac said as he began to pace. "They eat all the healthy hunts and leave the sickly stuff behind."

Mort paced in the opposite direction, passing Drac every few steps. "I knew they'd be trouble."

"It has nothing to do with the wolves." I didn't want Ethan

hurt after all he'd done to protect me, even if he was a bit moody. "I just . . . ate . . . I ate . . . cafeteria food."

"Oh, no! Not cafeteria food!" Drac fell to his knees.

Mort put her arm to her head in an overly-dramatic display of astonishment. "What have we done to deserve this?"

Surprisingly, this whole display was not them exaggerating or making fun of me. Cafeteria food was truly an abomination in their eyes.

"Peer pressure," I said, hanging my head low.

"I'm packing your lunch from now on." Mort stormed out of the room back into the kitchen and started clanging pots and pans around. She liked to cook when she was upset.

"Mort, I'm fine." I followed her into the kitchen. But I stopped in my tracks when I spied the mixer on the counter. My lungs sucked in air in a loud, gasping sound. "Not the mixer! No, not the mixer!"

"Oh it's time." Mort slipped her hand into a mitt.

"It's really not that bad. I'm fine. Really."

Drac stormed to the cupboards, opened the drawer and pulled out a beater.

"Don't do this!" I cried.

"We have no choice, Scarlet." He held the beater high in the air.

A sob built in my chest. The old suckers were going to bake a cake. "It's really okay. Everything is fine." But it was too late. Mort had already pulled the cake mix from the cupboard.

Drac beat the eggs, two at a time.

"Let us eat cake," Mort said, whipping the ingredients furiously. A bead of sweat formed on her brow.

Noooooo! Not cake! This was worse than I had ever imagined. They only baked cakes when they were upset. The last time she'd pulled out the mixer, I'd decided to make a snack of a security guard at the base.

Mort's cakes were the worst. She might have made the best pies on the planet, but her cakes were killers. Quite literally. She'd once accidentally poisoned an entire troop of soldiers.

I put my hand on Mort's arm. "It's not that bad. I promise."

Mort slowed, the muscle in her arm relaxing. "Are you sure?"

Wrinkling my nose, I said, "Yeah, I'm sure. I'm still full from the goodies I ate at Granny's house."

Mort shot up, surprised. "You've been eating sweets?"

Chapter 32

TARDY SLIP
☑ EXCUSED   Time 5min
☐ UNEXCUSED   Late
Scarlet Small

rac remained as cool as a cucumber. He glanced at
Mort and they did some more of that "eye-talking"
stuff. I wasn't sure if their frowns were because I'd
mentioned Granny or because of the sweets. "Scarlet," Drac
said slowly, "why don't you go upstairs and get ready for
school while Mort and I talk about this?"

I started for the staircase.

"Wait . . ." Mort's voice trailed off. I stopped. "Where did
you get that cape?"

Oh no! How could I ever explain this one? Could I tell the
truth? It was bad enough I had to tell them about my visits
with Granny. They'd freak out if they knew she gave me gifts.

"I . . . uh. . ."

The phone rang. Saved by the bell!

"Probably a problem at work," Drac said, grabbing the

phone. "I'll take it in the other room." With that he marched into the home office, closing the door behind him.

"I'm going to my room," I said.

By the time I came back down, the old suckers were engrossed in another whisper-conversation. Except this time I didn't listen to what they said. Instead, I snuck out the door before I was late for school.

When I arrived, most of the kids were already in homeroom and I whizzed past the front office, hoping no one would notice I was late.

"Tardy, Ms. Small!" Principal Petto placed his hand on my shoulder, pulling me to a screeching halt. My body quivered with fear.

"Eh, eh, eh." He waved a single finger, back and forth, like a slowly moving pendulum ticking away my doom. "Office first." He squeezed my shoulder, steering me toward the door. I tried to shake free from his grip but he only clutched tighter. For a wood-carving freak, he sure was strong.

"Okay, I got it." I wriggled free from his grasp. My undead heart trembled and thrummed in my chest. Mr. Petto gave me the creeps. I darted into the front office for my late pass, my lifeless body flustering with emotions. Anger at being bossed around, embarrassment for being called out on my tardy, but mostly fear. It's no wonder he was the principal. He could scare the living dead right out of a vampire!

With the tardy pass in hand, I made it to homeroom just in time to catch the tail-end of morning announcements.

Someone made a joke about the Cherry Pie Slaughter. It wasn't very funny, but I didn't really care. Mort and Drac knew about the skeleton. They knew about Granny. Worst of all, they knew about the wolf. They were going to force me to move. It was the first time I'd made friends, too, and my heart sank at the thought of leaving them.

At lunch, Cindy was seated in her usual spot when I wandered in. A girl named Vicki Larson sat at another table, her nose in the air like she was better than everyone else. "Hey, Cherry Face!" she called as I walked past.

Was that the best she could come up with? Cherry Face?

I plopped down next to Cindy, barely listening as she and Sarah jabbered the whole time.

"Have you seen Jen's new shoes?"

"I heard she got them at the thrift shop."

"Well, Daisy got braces."

"I heard her parents can't afford them."

My lifeless heart sank, heavy in my chest with everything on my mind, so I ignored the rest of their conversation, taking bites of my sand-witch and drinking my Bloody Tom with my elbows on the table. If Mort were there, she would have scolded me for bad manners, but I didn't care. On our way back from lunch, I overheard Sarah and Cindy say that they should go to the restrooms to try their new mascara.

"Do you want to come with us?" Sarah turned to ask.

My corporeal-challenged body froze. I knew what I

would see in the mirror. A non-reflection. I didn't want to be confronted with that. I couldn't let my friends see it either. That would be bad. Oh so bad.

Even if Mort and Drac were threatening me with another move to another town and a new school, I couldn't reveal anything to these girls. I still had to keep our secret. I owed them that much.

"Well, do you?" Cindy nudged persistently with her elbow.

"Um, no, you can go without me. I'm not a fan of makeup," I said smoothly.

"You should at least come with us. It'd be fun." Sarah really pressed my buttons without meaning to, so I took a deep breath to control myself.

"No, really, it's okay. I don't want to be late for math. My teacher is really picky." I added just to be positive I didn't make anything too obvious. The fact that Cindy was also in my math class didn't really occur to me at that moment.

"I guess you'll miss out on all the fun," Cindy said, winking at Sarah.

Oh, please. I would know this trick anywhere. To keep my cover, I pretended I fell for it. They sauntered off, and I called after them. "Wait up guys."

"I knew you'd come." Cindy beamed.

I gave her a stern glance. "Just this once."

The three of us shuffled to the restrooms. Cindy and Sarah went in, but I stayed in the doorway, avoiding the mirrors at all cost.

"Come on. We don't bite." Sarah laughed, gesturing to step inside. "Just try the makeup."

Peer pressure! Boy, how I hated peer pressure. "Nah, I'm good. I really don't like makeup all that much." I said as calmly as possible through shaking knees.

"Are you sure?" Cindy asked.

"Come on, Scarlet, it's not like there's anything to be afraid of . . . unless you're scared of your reflection," Sarah teased. "You're a real fright, you know?"

"Oooh, yeah," said Cindy mocking a damsel in distress, placing her arm against her forehead in a melodramatic way. "Remember the mess at the carnival? We had a real killer on our hands." Cindy pretended her index fingers were fangs. "Better watch out Sarah, she might be afraid because she's a vampire and doesn't have a reflection."

I gasped. My chest hurt as they both laughed. It wasn't really that funny. Even if Cindy was joking, was there part of her that believed I was a vampire? It was obvious from all the smart-alecky jokes that the pie-eating contest hadn't been forgotten.

My lungs quivered with breath. I couldn't give away my secret. I'd been challenged so many times lately. Between the pie-eating contest, the run-ins with the werewolf, and my visits with Granny, my life seemed to be spiraling out of control. What was with kids nowadays anyway? I never had this kind of peer pressure in the early 1900s.

VAMPIRE RULE #93
Never, ever fall victim to peer pressure.

Mort and Drac would kill me if they found out what I was about to do. This wouldn't end well for anyone . . . but I couldn't take the peer pressure anymore. Cindy and Sarah would see that I didn't have a reflection and they'd know that the mess at the carnival wasn't a joke. If they were my friends—my real friends—then they would understand and accept me, right?

I cleared my throat. Straightened my shirt. With Cindy and Sarah at my side, I marched up to the mirror, legs trembling, eyes closed tight. After bumping into the sink, I stopped. I opened my eyes, a pulse pounding in my veins. A row of shiny mirrors stretched out in front of me.

I blinked. Three reflections gazed back.

Chapter 33

Three beautiful reflections gazed into the mirror.

Cindy with her lovely blonde hair and big blue eyes.

Sarah, whose black hair with purple highlights made her hazel eyes even more beautiful.

And me.

I blinked.

No, that couldn't be! Three reflections? But Mort and Drac always said . . .

I blinked again.

Yup. It was true. There were three images, clear as day. I stretched my hand out and touched the glass.

My wide-eyed, quizzical face reflected back. My hair, nearly as black as night, swept to the side and around my face like beautiful wings. Dark, almond-shaped eyes that matched my hair were more of a defining feature than I'd ever known. Why had I hidden behind my bangs for so long?

I didn't know what to think since I was told vampires didn't have reflections. But I did have one. I leaned in close, inspecting myself for the first time in a century. Amazing! I hadn't changed a bit. I looked exactly like I did over one hundred years ago. I mean, I knew I hadn't aged, but it was remarkable just how perfect everything was. I was beautiful. Porcelain skin and perfectly shaped lips like little rose buds.

I tucked a strand of hair behind my ear, admiring myself.

"Wow, Scarlet." Cindy gawked. "You act like you've never seen your reflection."

"What . . ." I turned to answer her and that's when it happened. The mirror rippled like a pond when it starts to rain. I watched in horror as a new reflection appeared. The image of young, twelve-year-old Scarlet had vanished and was replaced with a wrinkled face and sunken eyes. Dark circles and gaunt cheeks. A sickly, horrid face revealed my worst nightmare.

I stumbled back, gasping.

Was that really my reflection gazing back? My hand touched the icy glass. It sure was my reflection and man was I ugly! And old!

"See, that wasn't so bad," Sarah said encouragingly, her hip popped to the side. She glided some Chapstick across her lips then smacked them together.

The wrinkled, old reflection continued to stare at me, disgusted, I stumbled backward another step, tripping on Cindy's bag. Catching myself before I slammed into the paper towel dispenser, I turned away, shielding my eyes from the reflection.

"Not so bad," Cindy said, "if it weren't for the random gravity check." She placed a hand over her mouth, giggling. "You okay, Scarlet?"

Wait. What was that?

I looked at them stunned. They didn't see the ancient, wrinkled face? Only I could see that? How odd. That must have been just one more thing the old suckers had lied to me about. Just another reason not to trust them. What else had they lied about all these years?

The bell rang, and I made a mad dash out of there.

VAMPIRE RULE #190

Don't knock down lollygaggers in the hallway. Even if it's on accident. It's a surefire way to get noticed. When you're trying to blend in, that's the last thing you want.

I made a quick stop by my locker to drop off my lunch box. While I was there I picked up my neglected math text book. I'd almost forgotten about it. I was just too upset.

We rushed off to class while I thought about what had just happened. I couldn't understand why I was the only one who could see my real reflection. At least now I knew I could use the restroom in school and not worry about being a reflection-free vampire. That was definitely good. It would have helped a few years back, when I'd drank too much fruit punch during lunch. Let's just say I never made that mistake again.

After school, I trudged home. Sarah ran ahead with Winnie and Bertha. Cindy stayed behind, her step even with my own.

"Everything all right, Scarlet?" Cindy seemed nice enough and certainly genuine but I wasn't used to sharing my thoughts, let alone my feelings, with other people. "You just seem a little 'off' today."

My bangs fell into my eyes as I turned to her. "It's just hard being the new kid." I brushed the hair out of my face. "Fitting in has never been my strength." She couldn't know about all the things in my life—I couldn't tell her. Not about the werewolf, or Granny or even the reflection I'd seen in the mirror.

"I think you fit in just great." It felt like she understood me so well, even if she really had no idea of what it was like to be an old-timey vampire living in a modern world. A vampire who was old as dirt, but trapped in a middle-schooler's body. A vampire who would probably never be taken seriously because of all the times she's messed up. A vampire who had loads of trouble trusting others, because she'd learned that others weren't to be trusted.

"Having you as a friend helps a lot." A lump formed in my throat after I said those words. I couldn't believe I'd actually admitted that. If I told her these things maybe that meant I learned to trust again. But why? And how? Maybe it was all because of Granny. Yes, Granny! I knew there was a reason I loved visiting her! She really helped me change.

"Wanna come over?" Cindy asked as we continued in step. It had become a game where we did a swivel with our hips and took a wide step out to the side. "We can do homework. Plus my step-mom makes a mean meat-lovers casserole."

As great as that sounded, I didn't really feel up to it. I really just wanted to go see Granny. "My parents are strict about school nights. Maybe another time." It wasn't a total lie—sometimes they were. Especially when I'd messed up and they grounded me forever.

When I walked through the door, Mort was putting on her coat.

"Where are you going?" It wasn't like Mort to go out in the middle of the afternoon.

"On a hunt," Drac said, appearing in the doorway of his office.

"But I thought you said 'no hunting'?"

"We didn't want you going out . . . it's not safe for little ghouls. But Drac can handle it," Mort said. "I'm going to be the distraction, should he need one."

"If we don't eat soon, none of that will matter." Drac laced up his shoes. "We'll all get into trouble when we eat something we shouldn't." He opened the door and cool air seeped in. "You stay put and we'll be back shortly."

Mort's eyes pleaded with me. "Be good, Scarlet. No more sneaking out."

The door clicked shut behind them and the silence became deafening. I didn't want to be alone—not now. I wasn't hungry for the meal Mort and Drac would bring home anyway. My mouth watered at the thought of Granny's sugary baked goods. It wouldn't hurt anyone if I went there to have another bite.

If I snuck out to see Granny, I could be back before they ever found out I was gone. They wouldn't have to know a thing. Eager to see her again, I suited up in my beautiful red cloak. I left my fedora on the table just in case I had another encounter with the wolf. I didn't need him ruining it again. With the house key tucked safely in my pocket I raced out the back door, through my yard and darted into the forest.

The trees stretched overhead in a carpet of leaves and branches. Thick bushes clawed at my arms as I shoved them out of the way.

The sound of wings flapped overhead. As I gazed into the hazy afternoon sky, bats looped in the air. An unusual sight, since bats aren't usually out during the day. "Shade," I called, stopping dead in my tracks. "Is that you? Where are you?"

A small black dot in the distance approached, growing larger and larger until he was inches from my head. "There you are!"

Shade beat his wings in response and landed on my head. Using his claws he crawled down my hair onto my neck until he had settled comfortably on my shoulder.

"Feels like I haven't seen you in forever. Shall we go to Granny's?"

He didn't speak, but I swore I felt him nod.

We traveled through the forest until a circular clearing appeared in the woods. Smoke puffed from the chimney of the little cabin and a fragrance of vanilla wafted through the air. It felt so warm and welcoming. Like I was finally home.

As usual, Granny sat comfortably on the wooden bench in front of her cottage, knitting with her large needles and ball of black yarn.

"Welcome back, dearie," she said when I stepped into the clearing. Once my foot touched the soft moss—sinking slightly beneath the weight of my boots—it felt like I'd arrived, safe and sound. "Isn't that cape just lovely on you?"

Blushing, I said, "Thanks Granny." Shade squirmed on my shoulder and I patted him.

Granny lowered her glasses to the tip of her nose. "Well, what do we have here?"

I stroked Shade's head. "It's a bat. I named him Shade."

She inspected Shade from a distance. "Umpf," Granny grunted, rising to her feet. It wasn't clear if her grunt was to my comment or because she struggled to stand. "I have something to show you, dearie."

Chapter 34

Granny toddled away, following the cobblestone path that circled her cabin.

Not missing a beat, I hopped in line behind her, curious as to what she would show me.

An uncomfortable stillness settled around us as we advanced in silence. The branches and leaves on the trees remained motionless despite a hefty breeze that threatened to lift me off the ground.

If I didn't know any better, I'd think that the trees were painted on the landscape, they were so still and unmoving. But I knew they were real. I'd just been in the forest and felt its branches for myself. The clouds hovered in place like a blanket over the moon. It made the sky darker than it should have been. But I kept going.

"Where are we going, Granny?" I took a step forward, my boot crunching on a branch lying on the ground. Another step and the mossy carpeted ground mushed beneath my feet, which made that branch seem so out of place.

Shade darted off, flapping his wings uncontrollably, bothered by the disturbance of the crunch.

"It's okay." I coaxed him down and he nestled into my neck. "It was just a twig." But I wasn't sure if I believed that myself, because when I took another step the sound of a second crunch made me nearly fall backward.

Crunch, crunch, crunch.

One more step, slowly, heavily, sinking into the soft moss with all my might. CRUUUUUUNCH! Impossible! The ground was soft as mush, nothing but moss and mud. Something else made that noise and it wasn't me.

My breath caught tight in my lungs. Don't turn around. Don't look!

Shade squirmed on my shoulder and I cast my gaze ahead. Granny's hair bounced like springs. Whatever that noise was, it couldn't be that bad. Granny would protect me.

At the end of the path lay a long wooden bridge, which crossed over a wide stream. It reminded me of my very first home, where I'd play outside, fishing, catching frogs and lizards and studying plant life hoping to make a wonderful discovery just like Charles Darwin. Thoughts of my pre-vampire days with my family came to my mind. Memories of easier, simpler times.

"Just a little farther, dearie." Granny stepped onto the bridge with hurried confidence.

One step onto the bridge and the whole thing wibbled

and wobbled. My hands gripped onto the handrail, afraid the whole thing would smash into the water at any moment. Shade flapped his wings, steadying himself. "Shhh. It's all right."

My unsteady gait made me stumble. Embarrassed, I blamed it on the bridge. "Dumb old thing," I muttered uselessly.

Thankfully Granny didn't see any of it. She led with intent, her curls springing on her head, completely oblivious to my random gravity check.

"What's that, dearie? Couldn't hear you all the way back there," she said in her slow, grandma-like voice.

"Nothing. It's just the dumb bridge tripped me," I confessed whole-undead-heartily, quickening my pace and taking my spot next to Granny.

She paused, wiped her spectacles and placed them back on her face. "Well, nice to see you, dearie."

"Uh, huh," I said, not knowing what else to say.

She grinned, her eyes hidden behind layers of wrinkled skin. "Be careful, I hear it has teeth."

"Teeth?"

"The bridge." She used her foot to flick something away. "Sometimes it likes to bite."

A large rabid-looking squirrel—or was it a raccoon?—raced straight to my feet. Three others were already busy gnawing my shoelace. "AAAHHHHH!!!" I shrieked. Shade dug his claws into my shoulder.

VAMPIRE RULE #194

When crossing a bridge with a granny-lady and creatures dare to shred up your laces, you don't have to tolerate it! Especially when you're wearing your best pair of Dr. Martins.

Jerking my foot away, one of the animals went flying, brown fur whizzing past and splashing into the water below. The rest scampered away, their bushy tails swishing behind them. "Ha ha. Teeth. Right," I said my voice shaking.

What was happening in Granny's forest? What had I just seen?

"Sometimes it likes to play tricks. Best to give it a treat when that happens." Granny placed a red and white striped dinner mint in the palm of my hand. "These are a favorite, but I understand they'll settle for a cookie on occasion."

My palm felt tingly and cool as though the mint were melting into my veins. I uncurled my fingers and saw the mint had been replaced with an ice cube. "What the . . .?"

Granny managed to get ahead again and I quickened my step to catch up to her. But as I tried to move, my left foot caught on something and I tripped, face planting on the wooden boards of the bridge. "Umpf!" It knocked the living-impaired breath right out of me and Shade went tumbling, landing a few feet ahead. I stood up and saw my laces had been tied together, and looped through another rope on the bridge. I rubbed my face. "Stupid bridge," I muttered as I patted my shoulder for Shade. He flew back, looking a little worse-for-wear, and settled in the crook of my neck.

"Rickety old thing, isn't it?" Granny called without looking back.

How'd she know? "Yeah, sure is." Feverishly, I untied the jumble of laces and ropes then darted to catch up with Granny. The bridge reacted to my tension, swaying with each step. I was beginning to think it had a mind of its own. It certainly wasn't a normal bridge, that was for sure. "So where are we headed, anyway?"

Wherever it was, I hoped we'd get there soon. We'd been on the freaky bridge forever! Frankly, I was growing tired and uneasy with rabid trick-playing squirrels who followed me, tying my shoes together and munching on my laces. Candy that turned into ice like a magic trick was more than I could handle.

"To the lake of dreams, dearie," she whispered, placing a finger to her lips. "But you have to be quiet or else the lake won't respond." She wrapped her shawl over her shoulders.

I rubbed my arms, thankful for the cape but chilled with thoughts that overtook my mind. When would I get some of Granny's goodies? My mouth watered at the thought of a cookie or a slice of pie. Heck, I'd give anything for a warm meal. Lamb stew sounded perfect. Funny, I usually just preferred lamb blood. What was wrong with me anyway?

Granny handed me a cookie that she seemed to pull from thin air.

"Thanks," I said before shoving it into my mouth. "Wait . . ." How did she know?

"Granny always knows, dearie."

A second later, we stepped off the bridge onto soft mossy grass surrounding a lake. The water extended as far as the eye could see. The moonlight sparkled on its surface and there was no end in sight for miles.

I glanced back across the bridge. It seemed to extend for miles when I crossed it, but now it appeared so small. Had it been my imagination? Were the wild animals real or had I imagined them as well?

"So, this lake of dreams . . . what does it do?" I held my breath waiting for an answer. When it didn't come, I added, "Does it predict the future?"

"Of course not, dearie. Don't be ridiculous." She grunted as she lowered herself on a carved log a few feet from the shore. "It shows your heart's greatest desire."

I snorted. As if that were any less ridiculous.

"Any desire?"

"No. Only your greatest one."

My heart leapt in my chest. My greatest desire? How would it know what that was when I wasn't even sure myself? And how could I be sure the lake would tell the truth if I didn't even know?

Chapter 35

"Here we are, dearie." Granny adjusted her skirt. "Go ahead. Look in."

"That's all I have to do? Just look in?" Bangs fell into my eyes as I tipped my head down, ready to gaze into the lake. "There are no magic words?"

"Well, no." Granny scratched her head, her curls springing with the touch. "Not unless you'd like to mutter something for the sake of it."

My heart fluttered in anticipation. "Not really." Was my greatest desire to have friends? Maybe it was to finally fit in. Or to have my parents trust me. Perhaps I'd like to stop moving around so much and just settle down in a forever home.

"Go ahead, dearie. No sense in waiting." She placed her hand in mine, squeezing it tight. It felt a bit too tight, but I didn't say anything.

Granny gave a gentle push, and I stumbled forward. As

soon as I fell, Shade flew off. Maybe he grew tired of my clumsiness. Regaining control I stepped cautiously, my toes curling inside my boots. With my eyes squeezed shut, I leaned forward. When I was sure I was close enough to see my reflection, I slowly opened my eyes.

In the water below, my face reflected back. Beautiful Scarlet Small. It was the same Scarlet I'd seen in the mirror at school with Cindy and Sarah. Dark eyes, dark hair that fell into my face and rosebud lips. I blinked a few times. That was it? I saw myself just as I am? That was my greatest desire?

"I don't get it." I backed away from the lake, my fists clenched in frustration.

Granny smoothed my hair. "Better check again," she whispered.

This didn't make any sense. But I stepped forward. This time I knelt on the bank, placing my palms on the cool soil, and leaned in close to the water's edge.

My reflection gazed back—wide eyes that didn't seem as happy as they used to be and a smile that seemed forced. Not at all the Scarlet I wanted to be. She looked too sad and much too lonely.

A breeze floated across the water. Goosebumps rose up on my arms, and the water rippled.

I heard Granny whisper something but I wasn't sure what it was, so I just watched the water.

The girl in the lake rippled. Soon, it changed to waves, and I couldn't see her anymore. I turned back, pleading with Granny desperately. This couldn't be all this stupid lake had

to offer. "I don't . . ." I began, my chest tight, a fire burning in my belly. A wind whipped across my skin and I spun toward the lake again. The lake stilled. It became as smooth as glass, as though I were peering through a window.

A hundred-year-old woman with wrinkles and saggy skin appeared. The same, pale complexion, dark hair and wide eyes. It was just like the reflection I'd seen at school.

My living-impaired breath caught in my throat. What was this trickery? I didn't like it one bit! I inched away, but Granny pressed her hand against my back. I wanted desperately to move.

The water rippled again and my youthful gaze smiled upon me. Except this time they flashed a pair of fangs. I touched my teeth with my finger. My fangs weren't out. They couldn't be, I wasn't ready to eat. But the reflection still showed me with fangs, pointy and sharp.

What was going on? I never wanted to be a vampire. That couldn't possibly be my greatest desire. My voice caught in my throat as I tried to object. This wasn't me! Not the real me!

My reflection flashed between the old lady, myself, and a fangified me. The images swirled and swirled making me dizzy and seasick.

A wretched, old lady, sharp, horrifying fangs, and beautiful, young me.

Old lady, sharp fangs, beautiful me.

Old, fangs, me.

My parents stepped into the background. They also

swirled from themselves to old, wrinkly faces, to fanged mouths.

Cindy's reflection appeared, too, flickering between her and a skeleton. Cindy, skeleton, Cindy, skeleton. Her image had a glitch, all static and fuzz. She had a secret. A skeleton curse. Something she'd never told me.

I watched skeleton-Cindy hide behind a bush, scare an old man, and run off laughing. She raced through a graveyard and was transported somewhere in a pink elevator. There was a skeleton mouse that seemed really cranky.

My heart pounded in my chest. Cindy and I were more alike than I could have ever imagined.

Ethan morphed from himself into a werewolf and back again. He howled in the bushes and chased a skeleton into a cemetery. In his human form he danced with Cindy. He ate pickled pigs feet. He put a skeleton foot back on Cindy's boney leg. I'd known his secret all along, but he was one of the good guys.

Which made me wonder . . . if Ethan was a good guy, helping Cindy, he wouldn't be mean to me (especially since he'd proven that at the school carnival). So why was he chasing me in the woods? Or . . . I gulped, pushing the thought into my stomach . . . if it wasn't him, then who?

Sarah changed too. A zombie. Just like the living dead, a corpse with rotting skin. I couldn't see anything else about her though. Maybe her story hadn't been told yet.

The images churned in the water, muddy bubbles

burping up from deep below. The lake became a mess of color and distorted faces.

I stumbled backward. What had I just seen? What was happening? My heart pounded in my chest until it nearly broke my ribs. My breath came in uncontrollable waves. I shut my eyes tight, trying to erase what I'd just seen, but the images haunted me.

When I caught my breath, I blinked and saw Granny hovering over me.

"Well, dearie . . ." She stretched out her hand. "What did you see?"

Truth was, I didn't know what I saw. I certainly learned things about my friends that I never thought I'd know. They definitely weren't what I thought they were.

Maybe I wasn't either.

She held out her hand and helped me up. Granny had a very strange expression on her face. Her eyes were wide with wonder. Her teeth clenched tight together behind a mischievous smirk. "Did you see your heart's greatest desire?"

"Yes. Yes, I did," I said as calmly as possible, trying to keep my voice even. A small quiver caught Granny's attention. The way she tipped her head gave it away.

"Well." Granny brushed her skirt. "We best be on our way."

Granny stayed behind this time, urging me to lead. I only glanced back once and I swore I caught a reflection in the lake that didn't resemble Granny at all. I wasn't sure what I saw—the image was too dark and distorted to make sense of it. But . . . if my mind wasn't deceiving me, I'd almost say I saw black, beady eyes and antenna growing from her head.

When I blinked, though, it was gone.

Chapter 36

"Would you like to stay for a treat?" Granny asked as soon as we reached her cottage.

Oh boy, did I ever want some of Granny's sweets! My stomach grumbled at the thought. But I needed to go home. I'd spent the entire afternoon with Granny, and dusk had already settled in. Plus Shade was nowhere to be found and I still felt terribly unsure about what I'd just seen in the water. "No thanks," I said, nervously surveying my surroundings. "I need to get home before my parents realize I'm gone. They'll be really upset."

"Oh. Of course you do." Granny grinned warmly. "Wouldn't want to worry them."

"Exactly!" It felt amazing to have Granny understand me. She'd been so kind to show me the lake of dreams, even if I wasn't sure about what I'd seen. "But I'll see you soon," I promised. I wanted to go back to the lake again, just so I could understand everything better. I'd never know what it meant with just one visit.

"Very soon," Granny urged, closing the door.

"Yes, Granny. Very soon." The urge to return grew stronger than I could imagine. My brain made a note of it like a strange obsession.

Eager to get home before the old suckers, my footfalls pounded on the ground as I ran through the forest. The last thing I needed was more trouble.

I knew the wolf was in the woods. I heard him. Smelled him. Swore he watched my every move, his glowing green eyes peeking through the brush. Or maybe they were yellow. I couldn't be sure anymore. Nothing seemed to make sense. There was the strange noise of thunder, and again I tried to ignore it as it rattled in my head.

Darkness threatened in the distance, but I wasn't scared. Not really. The cape would protect me, just as Granny had promised.

Something fluttered overhead. *Flap, flap, flap.*

"Shade!" I squealed. "I'm so glad to see you again!"

He beat his wings, blocking my view. Air whooshed in my eyes.

"What's wrong with you?" I shooed him out of the way. Shade continued to flap in front of me, not taking a single clue. "C'mon boy. On my shoulder." I patted my cape to urge him to land. He dived gracefully, nestling in the crook of my neck. "Good boy. Good boy."

I realized I sounded like I did when I talked to a dog. I

swallowed hard, nearly gagging at the thought of having a stinky dog for a pet. Especially one that smelled worse than the boys' locker room. Dogs make miserable companions. They chew up everything in sight and drool all over your brand new, one-hundred-dollar shoes.

Thinking of dogs made my head swim. Ethan's stench grew stronger and stronger. I sat down, feeling dizzy. As I leaned back against a tree, Shade flew off.

"Wait!" I called. "Don't leave." But as he flew off into the evening light I realized he'd come back when he was good and ready. Bats were funny like that. He'd always found me when he wanted. That was probably the closest thing I'd have to a relationship with him. It was good enough for me. I'd never had much luck with pets anyway.

VAMPIRE RULE #37

Animals never travel well. *sniff* Goodbye Terry the Tortoise. I'll miss you. You were the best turtle on the planet, even if you did bang your head into the tank every ten minutes.

Noises rustled in the leaves and my eyes darted toward the sound as a figure crept through the trees..

It emerged, and my pulse raced. A wolf! A huge, gray, mangy wolf. Its fur lay in matted clumps. Drool hung from its fangs. This was no ordinary wolf. No, it was a werewolf!

Ethaaaaan!

I knew I smelled him coming. It wasn't my imagination after all.

There was no need to be afraid since I had my awesome red cloak. "What do you want?" I said, plugging my nose. I couldn't stand to smell him a moment longer.

He kept his distance, remaining in the tree line a few feet away. It was probably because he was afraid I would go all awesome vampire powers on him and kick his sorry doggy behind.

A growl rumbled. "Scarlet, get out of the woods!" His eyes glowed yellow, reminding me of amber. Hadn't I seen amber eyes somewhere before?

My living-impaired breath caught in my throat. "What . . . what did you just say?" Was this the same wolf I'd seen before? I thought he'd had green eyes.

The wolf snarled his lip, exposing his teeth. "Get out of here and don't ever come back!" he snapped. The voice was thick and growly. He didn't sound like Ethan, but maybe werewolves sounded different when they talked in wolf form. I didn't even know they could talk to begin with.

Why would he care if I was in the forest? "I have every right to be here." I tried to hide the shudder in my voice.

I didn't like his attitude. "Besides, I'm on my way home anyway. What's it to you?" Although I wasn't going to admit it to him, I was super scared. In fact, my feet trembled in my boots, my beautiful scratch-free Dr. Martins. Granny said the cape would protect me, but so far this wolf didn't seem afraid of me. If he came too close, he might bite me and end my afterlife.

A low grumble started in his belly and shot through his

mouth in the loudest roar I'd ever heard. The wolf's yellow eyes glowed. It wasn't Ethan. I was sure of it.

If this wolf wasn't Ethan . . . then who was it? Maybe Ethan was a weird dog-boy, at least he'd help keep my vampire secret during the pie-escapade. So I figured he wouldn't really harm me. But this wolf? He wanted to hurt me. Bad.

Not wasting another second, I took off running, the wolf following close behind. His hot breath and heavy footfalls pounded on my heel.

My legs ached as my feet hit the ground with each frenzied step. My head became dizzy with each twist and turn through the thicket of bushes and trees. The leaves and branches swirled around me. Which direction had I come from? Where was I going? I couldn't tell. My mind—and the world around me—spun in a haze of disorientation.

Finally, not really sure if I could make heads or tails of where I was, I burst from the forest. "I'm not scared of you . . ." My breath came in fast waves. As I glanced back into the forest, the wolf had disappeared. I gulped. When had he stopped chasing me? And why?

The wolf's sudden disappearance made my hands shake in all the wrong ways. It put my vampire super senses on high alert and I leapt into the air, ready to take off into flight—

VAMPIRE RULE #196
How many times do I have to tell you? Vampires don't have super powers.

"Not afraid at all," I panted.

"Who are you talking to, dearie?" Granny asked.

"What?" I spun around to see Granny sitting on her bench. How did I get here? I'd been headed home before I . . . I'd gotten lost in the woods. After the strange bridge, the lake of secrets, and angry wolves, home was all I wanted.

Granny knitted again, with that same ball of black yarn and those same long needles. Glasses were perched at the tip of her nose, making her eyes huge. I never noticed how big they were before.

"You were talking to someone," Granny said, her eyes fixated on her knitting.

"Oh, that." I laughed. "Shade. He raced me." For some reason I felt like I shouldn't mention the werewolf that wasn't Ethan. I didn't know who he was, but he wasn't the decent doggy-fellow that Ethan was. This one would have bitten me and taken my afterlife if I'd given him the chance.

"Of course," Granny said, putting her needles down and folding her project in half. "Now . . . let's see . . ." She toddled to her front door, picked up a key from under the mat and unlocked the handle.

What an original hiding spot. Not.

"There we are, sweetie. Home sweet home." She said it with that sweet tone in her voice adults get when they're trying to be real polite. Usually it makes them sound like they're talking to a group of toddlers.

But it wasn't my home. Not really. My home was the one where my old suckers were, living their afterlife.

"Please do make yourself comfortable," she said as she squirmed and wiggled into a wooden rocking chair two sizes too small for her. "I'm so glad you've returned." Her voice dripped with sugary sweetness.

My nerves were on edge. What had happened in the forest? How did I end up back at Granny's? "Why thank you." I removed my cloak and set it on the couch. It landed with a soft whoosh, but I bet Granny couldn't hear it. She was too old and old people don't hear well.

"What was that, dearie?" Granny cupped a hand around her ear. Was it just me or had her ears suddenly grown double in size?

Granny cleared her throat. "Would you like something to eat?" She smiled, showing her large, white teeth.

I barely even heard her. It wasn't because I was such-an-old-vampire-I-lost-my-hearing either. It was because I was busy fixating my eyes at her abnormally large incisors. A horrible loud flapping sound shook me out of my wide-eyed gaping. I quickly glanced around the room. What could be making such a noise?

I nearly jumped out of my skin. There, resting on a nearby lamp, was a bat!

Chapter 37

She peered over the rim of her glasses. "Everything all right?"

"Oh . . . uh, yes. Everything is quite dandy." Dandy? Who was I? Sheesh.

I squinted. "Shade?" He flew off the lamp and flapped around the room. "How did you get here?" A very unsettling feeling swept over me. I wasn't even sure how to ask what I was about to say, so I blurted it out before I had a chance to think. "Granny, how'd you get my bat?" Well, he technically wasn't mine, but I felt like he was. "I mean, how'd you get Shade?"

Granny knitted furiously. "Well, dearie, I don't think . . ."

Shade sailed around the room, dive bombing us both like he'd lost his mind.

"It's a long story." Granny ducked out of the way as Shade took one last plunge before landing on a curtain rod. If I didn't know better, I'd almost say Granny seemed a bit nervous.

"Well . . . I've got plenty of time," I pressed.

Granny let out a long sigh. "Oh all right," she said with her sweet grandma voice, but it made my skin crawl. "Well, let's see." Granny scratched her head, thinking. "I was a young girl and I loved animals. One day I went with my friends to see some animals in their natural environment. Animals that hadn't been domesticated, hadn't been touched by the world, know what I mean, dearie?"

I nodded. I had seen too many animals harmed by the world, killed by hunters, struck by cars and . . . drained by vampires. My throat suddenly ached, whether from thirst at the thought of the tasty animals, or out of guilt from all the ones that had fed and sustained me during the last century, I didn't know.

Granny tipped her head, like she tried to understand my thoughts.

"Yes, I know what you mean," I said. "Go on." I had a feeling that I didn't want to hear the rest of her story. Something was a little strange and I couldn't put my finger on it. I wished I hadn't removed my cape. I reached for it, wrapping it around my shoulders.

"Well . . . my friends and I, we had made a list of all the animals we wanted to see in their natural habitats. One of them was a bat. So we snuck out after dark one night, the sky as black as Dracula's cape . . ." Granny stopped a moment. It was almost like her Dracula reference was deliberate.

VAMPIRE RULE #200

When wearing a cape, don't hide your mouth behind your arm, acting mysterious, with mysterious eyes and whip your arm down real fast revealing your fangs. A) You'll get a cramp in your arm. B) It's highly overdone. It might have been funny the first couple hundred thousand times, but it's not anymore. Trust me.

Granny's eyes lit with excitement. My body felt trapped in the chair, unable to move.

"Anyway, we had only the glow of a half-moon to guide our path. It was summer and the forest was alive with sounds of the night—locusts and crickets, coyotes and owls . . . wolves . . . all singing their music of the night." She gazed into the distance. "Even though the air was humid with summer heat, I felt a chill, and goose bumps rose up on my skin."

Was Granny a 'fraidy cat? Or was she trying to make me believe that so I'd feel sorry for her?

"As we entered the forest, we saw an entire family of bats, streaking through the sky, catching moths and bugs and soaring back into the trees to enjoy the fruits of their labor. But one of the bats . . . he didn't appear quite right . . . red eye . . . and his wing . . . The poor thing." Granny dabbed the corner of her eye with a tissue.

"Its wing was broken. So I approached slowly—I didn't want to frighten him. But the poor little creature, he just lay there, didn't even try to get away. After I scooped him up in my hands, I nursed him back to health. After that, bats seemed to swarm wherever I was. Shade is the great-great-grandchild of that very first bat. He's my good friend. Aren't you Shade?"

Shade moved on the curtain, beat his wings and soared through the room. He landed on Granny's shoulder and clawed his way to her neck.

"I trust him with everything." Granny grimaced. "Even with . . ." She paused, handing me a plate of cookies.

I gulped. Hard. She didn't need to finish her thought for me to know things weren't quite right. Why had Shade found me in the forest on all those occasions? Maybe it wasn't because he wanted to be my pet after all. Maybe he was . . . no. I shook my head. It couldn't be. But the thought came back to me. Nothing else made sense. Shade was Granny's spy. But why?

Reluctantly, I reached for one of the cookies. I had to act normal, like I didn't know anything. The cookie moved, scurrying away from my grasp. "Uh . . . no thank you."

"Well, if you're so sure," Granny said, holding a wiggly cookie between her fingers. She crunched into it, grinning as crumbs dropped to the floor. When the crumbs landed, they broke into smaller pieces and scurried away. Had all the cookies I'd eaten at Granny's done that and I'd just never noticed? My stomach churned at the thought, holding its very own revolution.

Vampires really shouldn't have such weak stomachs. It's not so great for the whole survival instinct. But I knew it wasn't a cookie she ate. Whatever it was, I decided, was not something I wanted entering my abdominal cavity.

When Granny finished the very last morsel of her so-called cookie, she brushed the crumbs off her lap and wiggled free from the chair. She stood with a grunt and bustled off to the kitchen.

Reluctantly, I followed her. Even if things seemed strange, I'd be safer at Granny's than the forest with that wolf. So far, at least, she hadn't tried to hurt me.

Granny rifled around in the cabinets, making a whole lot of ruckus. A few moments later, she placed a hand on her hip. Her back cracked as she straightened in excitement, holding something high in the air. "Here it is!" She waddled her way back into the living room. "My old cooking pot. You know, Shade always loves a good chocolate ladybug cookie."

Granny took a spice jar from the cupboard. She opened the top and dumped three hard shakes into the pot.

"Ladybugs," she said as a few of them flew out of the pot, which reminded me a little too much of a cauldron, if you asked me.

My throat felt tight. A little old lady in the woods. A pet bat. A cauldron. It added up to something that I didn't want to admit.

Granny hummed merrily, "Over the river and through the woods."

Her song rang in my ears as I quietly slipped out of the kitchen into the living room. Wolf or no wolf, I had to get out of here.

As I snuck through the living room, a wall of photographs caught my attention. Black and white portraits, all framed in various shapes and sizes. Why hadn't I noticed them before? Generations of different people all posed with straight faces. But some of the photos, the people wore strained expressions, as if they were trying too hard. Oddly, I didn't see Granny in a single photograph. Or maybe I just didn't recognize her.

I scanned along the wall, studying the photos. Something wasn't right about any of this. My eyes fell on three separate photos, hung neatly in a row. My undead heart thumped wildly. Each portrait was from a different time period, but the face was the same in every photo.

A girl with dark hair. They all had the same almond shaped eyes. The same tell-tale rose bud lips. In fact, I even recognized one of the dresses. I used to wear it all the time before Mort made me give it up in order to fit in.

My skin prickled like thousands of little needles as a realization dawned on me. It was as if I were looking in a mirror.

The girls were me!

Chapter 38

Granny had portraits of me throughout my vampire life. She knew I was a vampire. That meant she wasn't who I thought she was. This little old lady was worse than a witch.

Granny strolled into the room and I gasped, which I quickly covered by faking a yawn. I couldn't let her know I knew anything. Not yet. I had to play along. Because if I was right and Granny was who I thought, then games were a favorite. And so were sinister plans. Losing would mean my afterlife.

Her face grew mischievous, and my hands dripped with sweat. "I better be on my way now." My voice quivered even though I tried really hard to keep it even.

"Why such a rush, dearie?" Granny reached for my hand but missed and clutched my wrist tight in her grasp. Her eyes lit as she felt my cold dead skin. "No need to hurry off."

"It's l-l-late . . ." I jerked out of her grasp. "Th-thanks for th-the cookies. The-they w-w-were delicious."

"But you haven't even tasted any cookies yet." Granny swirled around, taking me with her. She grabbed a light colored wicker basket from the side of the fireplace. She shoved it at me, pushing it into my belly. The checkered blanket covering the top of the basket wiggled and squirmed. "Eat up."

My mind raced, my afterlife flashing before my eyes. I thought about Ethan. He hadn't been after me. Wolf-boy had been trying to warn me. All those times he'd growled and chased me in the woods were a warning, trying to deter me from Granny's house. But I didn't listen. I was too stubborn to take advice from some smelly dog. Actually, I was just too stubborn to trust anyone, let alone a werewolf. Besides, what could he have known about sweet old Granny who made cookies for her pet bat and made me feel welcome? He was wrong about her, wasn't he?

I shook my head. No, I was the one who was wrong. All this time I'd thought she helped me, but she just lured me into her evil plans.

What about that other wolf? Was he trying to help me? Or was he Granny's spy, just like Shade?

"Go on." Granny pushed the basket into my stomach again. I stumbled but caught myself before I fell. "Eat up. You wouldn't want to miss all those yummy sweets, now would you, dearie." Granny tipped her head back and cackled, her soft pearly white teeth changing into rotten, brown lumps.

My hand shook as I pulled back the red and white checked blanket. Black insects scurried out. Millions of legs twitching, hard shells and exoskeletons clicking, creaking, screeching. They raced up my arm, straight to my neck.

I threw the basket, my heart pounding in my chest. "Nooooooooo!" I screamed. The bugs scuttled straight to my mouth. I promptly closed my lips muffling my scream. But I wasn't fast enough. A bug had crawled inside my mouth. Its legs scratched my tongue, pinched the inside of my cheeks. "Owh!" I yelled, spitting the putrid thing across the room.

More bugs scurried toward my mouth but I closed my lips in time. They altered their direction, swarming toward my nostrils. My muffled scream came through tight lips as millions of bugs covered every inch of my body. They squirmed in my hair, itching my scalp like lice. They covered my eyes, so my world became nothing but blackness. I collapsed to the ground in a black heap, swatting and batting, flicking and smashing.

I swatted them off my face and screamed. "Heeelp! Someone help me! Please!" The bugs found their way into my open mouth and I choked, gagging and spitting them out.

I was drowning in a pool of black insects. No one would ever know. I'd die a painful afterdeath . . . all alone. But I wouldn't die without a fight.

Fear and anger consumed me and my fangs popped out. I hissed. Bugs scrambled away from my face. They crawled to my hair, their tiny legs tangled in each strand.

Shade flew off Granny's shoulder, dive bombing me.

"Leave me alone!" I swatted him away. But Shade persisted, and he swooped down once more. "Go away!" I shouted, still crushing bugs. I was in enough trouble with the millions of bugs biting and clawing at my skin.

A growl rumbled from Granny. "SHAAAAAADE!" she screamed, stomping her feet, her face turning a strange color of purple-ish-red.

Shade ignored her as he plunged again, grabbing one of the bugs and eating it. If I didn't know better I'd think he wanted to help. Why would he do that? He was clearly Granny's spy, sent to gain info and lure me into her trap. Even if he did intend to help, there were way too many insects for just one bat to handle.

"Good boy, Shade." I managed to mumble as bugs scurried toward my face again. He must have been happy with my praise because he kept at it, diving down, eating a bug and flying off, over and over again.

Granny's fury ignited, smoke escaping her ears as she held her breath. She stomped a foot on the floor, rattling the whole house. She stomped the other foot. The sound echoed like the boom of fireworks. The floor rattled and I leapt to my feet, still swatting at bugs.

A deep guttural sound grew from Granny, building in the pit of her stomach. It spewed from her mouth with a thunderous roar. She threw her head back, her rotten teeth protruding from her gums. As if she'd commanded an army, the walls of the house squirmed.

The bugs suddenly changed direction and crawled out

of my hair, down my face, scratching and clawing on their way. They quickly scurried off, running into the floorboards and under the windowsills. In a flash, they all disappeared. All but one. I flicked the last bug off and Shade swooped down and gulped it up.

The walls squirmed as if they were alive. They moved in a giant wave. One by one, piece by piece, the walls came apart, dividing into a million colorful bats.

They'd been disguised as furniture and draperies, blending into their surroundings like a chameleon.

As they flapped, the colors flew off their wings in a cloud of rainbow colored dust. Soon the bats took on shades of brown and black. The ceiling lifted into a moving, breathing cloud of darkness. The flapping of all their wings became deafening. I covered my ears and fell to my knees. They swirled and flew, tunneling around me like a tornado into the eye of the storm. I was trapped inside a giant bat vacuum!

Granny inched away. The buttons of her dress popped off like kernels of corn. She twisted, writhing like a lizard hatching from inside an egg. Her chest split open, slime and pieces of shell bursting across the room. A bug-like man emerged, sticky with goo. He held a cane in one hand, supporting his seven other jagged, bug-like legs. Antennae protruded from his head. His dark, buggy eyes were the same ones I'd seen in the lake of secrets.

I would know him anywhere. I'd met him once before when I died and turned into a vampire. His angry face, no matter how he'd disguised it, was unmistakable. This

creature was Mr. Death and he'd come from the Underworld to take me away. He warned me long ago that undead things belonged in the ground—dead and buried.

Mr. Death scuttled closer, the swarm of bats still swirling around us, the sound as loud as a freight train.

"What do you want?" I shouted. I was sure he couldn't hear me, and even if he could, Mr. Death answered to no one.

With a snap of his fingers the bats dissipated, covering the night sky like a moving blanket of darkness.

Mr. Death pulled knitting needles from behind his back and the black blanket that he'd knit (disguised as Granny) fell to the ground. He shook the blanket and it unrolled in front of me. The intricately woven design revealed a giant spider web. The ground trembled like an earthquake. It shook and made great groaning noises. I stumbled forward. The ground quaked, opening into a massive sinkhole.

Chapter 39

My feet were frozen in place. Run, Scarlet, run! But I couldn't move. Fear paralyzed me. My stomach heaved.

Mr. Death scuttled forward, his ugly buggy body making me quiver.

My legs wobbled as Mr. Death grabbed me around the waist with his giant sticky bug legs. He pulled me into the web.

"Nooo!" I screamed, flailing. Overhead, just inches away, Shade beat his wings, circling. I wanted to tell him to get help, to get Cindy and Ethan, and maybe even my parents. But I couldn't risk Mr. Death hurting them too.

Seeing my distress, Shade swooped down, but as he got close Mr. Death batted him away. Shade spiraled out of control and slammed into a tree. He fell to the ground and lay there lifeless.

My heart sank. He was my only hope. Now he was gone forever.

"I never did like that bat," Mr. Death said, shooting silvery threads from his wrists and tying my hands into his carefully crafted web.

I struggled to break free, but his threads were too strong, the web too sticky. Mr. Death scurried along the edges of the web, which centered over the giant hole in the ground. He released the threads one by one, the web bouncing dangerously over the hole, which threatened to eat me alive. I peered down into nothingness. If he released all of the corners before I could escape, I'd be swallowed up by the hole in the ground, taken to the Underworld, never to be heard from again.

I turned my wrists, trying to slip one of them free. Mr. Death fumed. "You'll never escape!" He scurried along the web, tearing the edges away. "You're going back to the Underworld where you belong." He cackled like a witch. It made him sound like a girl, not a menacing man.

"You'll never take me alive." I realized what I said too late. I technically wasn't alive, and I hadn't been for a very long time.

"It's a good thing you're already dead, Scarlet Small." He titled his head back again, laughing maniacally. A bug scurried out of his mouth.

The threads burned my wrists as I tried to escape. "I'm not going with you. I belong here!" I couldn't believe I'd uttered those words. I'd never felt like I'd belonged anywhere

in my entire afterlife. "I have friends . . ." a tear escaped from my eye ". . . and they'll come looking for me." My face dripped with tears. My cold heart felt warm with emotions.

"Ha! You don't have any friends. You never did. You're a lonely, pathetic girl. Your parents don't even care about you. Look at you. You're nothing but a sorry excuse for a vampire."

He'd said what I'd thought so many times. I was pathetic. I was . . . I used to be . . . but now? Now I was strong. I had a family. Mort and Drac cared about me. I'd even made friends. I couldn't give up. Not now. Not ever. Not in a million undead years. "You don't know anything about me."

"You were so desperate, you had no choice but to seek the friendship of an old woman." He dropped down on his knees, snipped a thread from the web and it swayed, my body bouncing like a child on a trampoline. "Someone who filled your belly with sweets." Mr. Death took another piece of web in his nasty bug hands, this time putting it to his mouth and biting it with his teeth. "You thought those sweets made up for being lonely and lost."

Mr. Death picked up another strand of the web, bouncing it in his palm, taunting me with it. My life clung to just a few remaining strands of thread. He dropped the piece from his hand. The web swayed in place, my body swaying, making my head spin. I felt like someone who'd been at sea for too long. But I slowly and carefully wriggled a wrist. It was my only chance to break free.

"Instead, those sweets just made you more useless and

feeble." He laughed, this time a deep guttural sound, more appropriate for the bug-like creature he'd become.

"I'm not useless." My wrist slipped out of the tacky threads binding it to the web. "Or feeble."

Another laugh. "Don't you see? I laced all those treats with blood. With each and every bite, each tasty morsel, you became more and more dependent on an old woman to make you happy. You needed me. I supplied all the nourishment you needed for your afterlife."

"I trusted her!" My stomach burned with betrayal as I thought about how much I enjoyed Granny's treats, how she'd made them just for me. "I trusted you!" I couldn't believe I'd been so stupid. I should have trusted the people who really mattered in my life. The ones who cared about me. My parents. Cindy. Ethan. Sarah.

"Then I succeeded." Mr. Death was so busy insulting me he didn't notice I'd slipped both of my hands from the web. "I won."

"No!" I sat up, my hands free from his trap. "I did." I leapt up, the last half a dozen strands of web supporting my weight.

Mr. Death's jointed jaw dropped in shock. "We'll see about that!" He snipped some more strands, leaving only three threads hanging. The web slipped open like a trapdoor.

And I fell.

Chapter 40

I grabbed onto anything within my reach. As the web collapsed into a wall of dirt, I wrapped a piece of it around each wrist, saving myself from an indefinite freefall.

My face ached as it collided with the side of the hole. Soil and pebbles fell into my hair, puffs of dirt wafted into my face. It filled me with an earthy smell, reminding me of Cindy, and I longed for my friend.

The web vibrated. Mr. Death's beady eyes glared down into the hole. "You're not dead yet?" he mocked with a laugh as he clipped one of the three remaining strands. The web shook and I held on for my dear undead life, struggling not to fall. The Underworld glowed below in an eerie light. Carnival music flooded my ears with creepy, bell-like tones. I couldn't be trapped there! I just couldn't. I had too much waiting for me here. Too many people who loved me.

I climbed the web, clinging to it. But it clung back, sticking to my clothes, shoes and hands like chewed up bubble gum. Mr. Death clipped the second to last piece of web. "It's quite a ride," he cackled. "Hold on tight!"

"I'm not going anywhere!" I gripped the sticky threads and with each struggled climb, a bit of the night sky glittered with stars, beckoned above. It gave me hope and my heart warmed. A feeling I hadn't experienced in a long time filled me. I just had to get out of the hole. I couldn't go to the Underworld.

Mr. Death scuttled to the very last piece of web, gripping it with his scissor-like claws. A thunderous crash sounded somewhere deep in the forst. Mr. Death's buggy eyes grew wide and he dropped the webbing. He backed away, the clicking of his insect legs reminding me of the millions of bugs he'd launched on me.

Maybe he thought I was dead for real this time. Or maybe he was just as afraid of the crashing noise as I was. Either way, it was my chance to escape.

I climbed, hand over hand, holding onto the web, using it to help me to the surface. I'd only moved a couple of inches, when I glanced up to see Mr. Death's face glaring over the edge of the hole. "You're not getting out of there alive, Ms. Small." He raised a limb above his head then pointed. "Get her!" Mr. Death scuttled away and creatures with glowing red eyes scrambled down into the hole. I recognized them as the rabid squirrel-like animals that attacked my feet on the bridge! Within seconds, they were on me, tearing at my clothes, gnawing my shoes. I batted one away as it scratched

my face, narrowly missing my eye. My hand slipped, but I grasped more web before I fell. Another creature hissed near my face and I balled my hand into a fist, making contact with its head. It hit the opposite wall and plummeted into the Underworld.

Before I had a chance to recover and nurse my wound, another creature replaced the first. A third clawed its way up my torso, its razor sharp teeth dripping with venom as it struck my neck.

Batting one with my fist, tears streamed down my face, as it tore the flesh from my hand.

I was going to die.

Desperate and helpless, I screamed out. "Someone help me! Please!" My breath was heavy with fear. Gazing up into the night sky, I realized I was alone. No one would ever hear me. I had to solve this problem myself. Couldn't depend on someone else.

Mustering all the strength I had left, I kicked and lashed out until only one persistent demon-squirrel remained. My arms burned—I couldn't hold on any longer. I spied a ledge just a few feet above me. If I could make it there and rest I'd be able to get rid of this last one. I cringed as I let go of the web, hoping I'd be able to make it to the ledge without falling. Hand over hand, feet scrambling to help, my head jerked as the last squirrel-creature bit my ear, sending pain searing through my head.

My fingers ached and dirt caked beneath my nails. The promise of the ledge beckoned within my reach. I reached for it, but the rabid squirrel scratched at my head, tearing a wad of hair from my scalp. Batting the evil thing away, my hand collided with the ledge. I gripped on, pulling myself to safety. Once balanced on my feet, I grabbed the squirrel by the tail. His razor teeth pierced my hand. Yelping, I shook my hand, but the squirrel's tooth broke off and he sailed through the air.

Panting from pain and fear, I slumped against the wall of the dirt hole. The opening was so close, I could smell fresh air, see the trees. I climbed up, my hands burning, dirt caking my palms. Blades of grass danced along the edge of the hole. Finally! As I touched the grass, feeling its soft blades, a skeleton hand gripped mine.

"Nooo!" I screamed. It couldn't be! I'd come so far. The Underworld was far away. I couldn't be taken down by a skeleton.

"Quiet," the voice whispered. "Or he'll come back."

"You can't take me down there!"

"Scarlet! Be quiet," a voice growled. It sounded familiar. Ethan?

A skeleton face regarded mine, wide eyed, peeking over the edge of the hole. "Scarlet, it's Cindy," she whispered.

It smelled like Cindy, but could I really be sure? Could I trust her? Or was this just another trick by Mr. Death?

"Prove it," I demanded, dangling by my fingertips. Now wasn't really the best time to argue with anyone, but I couldn't be tricked again.

Another head scrutinized me over the edge of the hole.

"Scarlet," the wolf growled, his green eyes glowing like precious gems. "Would you just take her hand and climb out of there already?"

"Ethan? Is that really you?"

A second wolf growled, his yellow piercing eyes, peering down at me. My body shook with fear. Two wolves? Ethan was the good one. The one who helped me. But this second wolf, he'd chased me in the forest straight to Granny's. He was part of Mr. Death's plan.

"It's just Hunter," Cindy whispered. "He's here to help, too."

Hunter? Of course Hunter was a wolf. He and Ethan are brothers. Why hadn't I realized that sooner? "But he tried to kill me." I gulped. "In the woods."

Chapter 41

"He tried to help," Cindy said. "Ethan told me you weren't listening to him, so he sent his brother." Ethan howled in agreement, then nudged his brother with his muzzle.

"He thought maybe you'd listen to Hunter instead." Cindy scratched behind Ethan's ear. "They've been trying to keep you away from Grandmother's house."

"But you got so disoriented, you landed right into Mr. Death's trap," Hunter said.

I trusted Cindy . . . and I even trusted Ethan . . . But Hunter?

Cindy reached her other hand out to me. "C'mon. We've got to get you out of here before it's too late."

Clutching onto her hand, she pulled me up with Ethan and Hunter's help. They had their drooly muzzles wrapped around each of Cindy's ankles, dragging us both in the process.

When I could lift myself the rest of the way, I hoisted my legs out of the hole and onto the grass. Exhausted and unbalanced, I struggled to stand.

Cindy tackled me to the ground. "I've been so worried about you," she cried. "Don't ever pull a stunt like that again!"

Ethan and Hunter nudged me with their muzzles. It was the first time I was happy to have a cold, wet dog nose pressed against my cold, dead skin. I guess we did have something in common after all.

"But ... how did you know? I mean ..." My breath came in waves, exhaustion taking its toll. "How did you know where to find me?"

A bat fluttered overhead. "Shade?" He dived down and landed on my shoulder. "You brought them back to help me, didn't you?" His little head nestled into my neck and I knew it was true.

In between the trees something moved. Mr. Death? My breath froze in my lungs. Mr. G. Petto stepped from the forest, an ax swung on his shoulder. Behind him, he dragged logs and tree limbs with chains.

"We had some help from Principal Petto, too," Cindy said. "He came to the forest to chop wood, and heard all the screaming."

"That's right." Mr. Petto stepped let the chains drop from his hand. "But I tried to help before that. I attempted to stop you after the carnival, but you just had to follow Granny into the woods, didn't you?" Mr. Petto ran his hand across his bald head. "I did everything I could to keep you out of trouble—making you clean up after the carnival, giving you tardy slips."

"Don't forget detention!" I said.

Mr. Petto shook his head. "No, you did that one all on your own. Can't stay out of trouble for a single moment, can you, Miss Small?" He put his ax down, so it stood upright, resting his elbow on the handle. "I even chopped down trees in the forest, hoping the thunder would scare you home. . ."

Noise rustled in the woods before I could respond.

"Let's get out of here," Ethan growled. Cindy jumped onto his back. Hunter urged me to follow suit. Reluctantly, I gripped a clump of his fur and climbed on.

"Not so fast," a voice rumbled. Mr. Death lumbered into the clearing. "I thought I got rid of you!" He pointed his jagged insect leg at me.

"You'll never get rid of me." I gave Hunter a nudge. "Time to go," I whispered.

Mr. Death's face contorted, anger seething from him. He grew, his size doubling . . . tripling . . . until his head leveled with the tops of the trees. His antennae twitched in the treetops. His body shook, until he fully transformed into the ugliest bug-like creature I'd ever seen, a beetle-like abdomen and pinchers the size of a small car. "You're coming to the Underworld if I have to take you there myself!" He stomped all eight of his legs the width of tree trunks, making a sound like thunder.

"I told you, I'm never going with you!"

Ethan dashed off, Cindy clinging tightly to his back.

"Ah," Mr. Death proclaimed. "I see you've brought your friends. I'm particularly interested in a skeleton girl who visits her mother in the Underworld." He shot a spidery thread from his chest at Cindy. It wrapped around her ribcage, pulling her from Ethan's furry back.

"Help!" Cindy screamed.

Mr. Death retracted the thread and brought Cindy up to his giant face. "Maybe you'll just be lunch instead. I've always had a fondness for bones." Mr. Death's massive mouth pinchers snapped in front of Cindy's face, threatening to tear her to pieces.

"No! Not my friend!" I screamed. She really was my friend, wasn't she? "Take me instead." I leapt off Hunter's back and ran over to one of Mr. Death's giant, tree-stump legs. I climbed it, scurrying up to the first joint. Mr. Death kicked me off, and I flew through the air, landing against a tree, banging my head.

"Oh. I came for the skeleton girl all along." Mr. Death cackled. "Don't you see, you useless excuse for a vampire?"

I rubbed the back of my head.

"Once you saw your reflection in the lake, I knew Cindy was your friend. I suspected it all along, but I needed proof." His antennae flicked as if they sensed trouble. "When that naive little brain of yours believed everything was real, I knew I could trick you into just about anything. As soon as I saw her reflection with yours it was just a matter of time before I'd have her in my grasp." He twitched his pinchers, threatening to crunch Cindy's bones in one giant snap. "I just had to keep luring you in with treats and goodies. Eventually your friend would come to save you. I know her type all too well."

Ethan and Hunter bolted to Mr. Death, their teeth gnawing on his legs as if they were giant bones. Mr. Death gave a swift kick and they both went flying through the air. They both yelped when they landed.

I had to save Cindy. She needed my help. She was my first friend in a really long time, but I knew one thing. Friends do all they can for each other.

My eyes darted from the logs Mr. Petto had dropped on the ground, to the ax he steadied his elbow on. I had an idea. "Mr. Petto," I called. "I hear you like to carve wood." I tipped my head toward his ax. He gave the slightest nod, as if he understood.

Then I ran.

When I reached the hole I leaned over and glanced down into the darkness. The Underworld glowed below, but Cindy needed me.

So I leapt into the hole.

Chapter 42

Ethan and Hunter howled above me. It was the saddest sound I'd ever heard, and I knew they were mourning for me. Their friend.

I fell. Down, down, down. I grabbed onto a stray tree root, my body slamming hard against the soil of the hole, my arm nearly yanking out of the socket.

Clinging there, my body aching in pain, I waited. Would Mr. Petto be able to do what I'd asked?

I couldn't tell what was happening up there, but I could hear wails and cries.

But then I heard it. A very distinct sound. An ax striking wood, chopping and chopping. The same noise I'd heard in the forest all those times before. Mr. Petto understood what I'd asked of him. He chopped Mr. Death's wood-like legs, taking the monster down!

The sound reverberated within the walls of the hole like

thunder. If my plan worked, Mr. Death would fall into the hole at any moment, like a tree falling in the woods. This was it. The moment of truth.

"Timber!" Mr. Petto called.

I scurried up the dirt walls, groping for tree roots, rocks, anything. There wasn't much time to get into position. And I'd have to be careful. Still clinging to the roots, I pressed myself tight against the soil, gazing into the opening above me.

With a final crack and a smash, Mr. Death fell, his ginormous body crashing down the hole. His black, beady eyes changed into flames of red that lit the cavernous hole as he plunged down.

He kept Cindy tucked under one of his broken, log-like legs. She squirmed and writhed to break free. When she saw me, her eyes lit up. Her boney hand shot out, stretching toward me. I grabbed it and pulled her from Mr. Death's grasp.

Cindy dangled from my fingertips as Mr. Death flailed, falling down the massive hole, his variegated abdomen facing us, like a turtle on his back.

"I've got you," I grunted, pulling Cindy with all my strength.

"Just don't let go," she said, reaching up with her other hand and gripping my wrist.

My arms ached, but Cindy swung her body, her boney toes gripping onto a tree root. She bore her weight there, easing the burden on my arm. I made my way to the same small

ledge that had saved me from the rabid squirrel-creatures. I helped Cindy onto it, her bones clinking and clunking. We clung to each other, hugging, our bodies trembling with exhaustion.

Mr. Death became nothing but a darkened speck backlit by the glow of the Underworld

"Hurry," I said. If Mr. Death was able to stop his free-fall, he'd make his way back up the hole. As soon as he found us, he'd drag us to the Underworld for sure. "We don't have much time. We have to get out before he figures out a way to stop us."

Darkness loomed both above and below us. We struggled up the walls of the hole, clinging to dirt and roots, hardened soil and rocks.

"Look!" Cindy pointed toward the entrance of the hole. The sky above us glistened. Not only could I see the sky, but morning sparkled like a welcome friend. Cindy's body transformed from the skeleton into the girl I'd always known from school. The girl who would always be my friend, no matter what form she took.

The sun's ray struck me, and I squinted, losing my balance. Cindy grabbed my hand. "C'mon Scarlet," she urged. "Just a little farther. We're almost there."

As we approached the top, two faces peered down into the hole. My parents!

"Scarlet." Mort started crying. "Oh Scarlet."

Drac's face crumpled with relief when he saw me. "Grab on!" they said together, throwing a braided rope into the hole.

Cindy grabbed onto the dangling rope. She pulled it down, knotting it around our waists. "Ready!' She gave the rope a tug and it jerked us up.

Exhausted, I collapsed on the ground, just as it began to rattle and shake.

"Things unseen, remain hidden," Hagatha recited.

"What?" I turned to see Cindy hugging her dad.

Hagatha chanted, with arms crossed, a purple haze glowing in a dome over the hole. It danced with a rainbow of color and a whisper of a breeze blew my bangs from my face. The hole sealed up instantly and grass appeared. It appeared as though the battle had never occurred. One last grumble rattled from deep in the ground, like a volcano ready to erupt. I braced myself, squeezing my eyes shut tight, for Mr. Death to appear but I felt someone squeeze my arm.

"You're safe now," Hagatha assured us with a calm voice, and I felt like I'd known her forever. She was kind and good and not at all like I'd thought a witch would be. I silently vowed never to eat another sandwitch again.

Mr. Petto leaned on his ax at the edge of the forest. He waved, a pool of sweat dripping from his bald head. I waved back, thankful for his help, even those times it meant I got in trouble.

A bat soared through the sky. "Shade?" I whispered. He dove down and nestled into my neck. "Oh, Shade, how can I ever thank you?"

Mort and Drac smiled wearily. They probably knew

where this would go. I had a feeling their strict no-pet policy would be lifted. Just this once.

"How did you know where to find me?" I asked my parents.

"We had some help." Mort tipped her head toward Ethan.

"I did too." I glanced around, but Mr. Petto had disappeared. The only thing that remained was his ax. The shiny metal of the blade reflected rays of sunlight, bouncing among the trees.

Drac saluted. "These boys are good friends, Scarlet. I'd trust them with my afterlife."

Drac and Mort wrapped their arms around me, hugging me tight. I pressed my head into their bellies, unwilling to move.

"Thanks for helping our little ghoul," Mort said. The old suckers opened their arms and Cindy collided into me. They circled their arms around her, hugging her tight. Ethan and Hunter squeezed between us, nuzzled their noses into our arms and slobbered on our clothes. No complaints from me.

Roger and Hagatha looked on from the sidelines. My parents waved them over and Drac, who never let go of his military bearing, pulled them into the circle.

What would I have done without my friends? I squeezed them all back, wishing the feeling would never end.

VAMPIRE RULE #250
Friends are cool. And epic. And beast. They're so beast!

acknowledgements

Many thanks to the special people whose support made this book possible.

My rawking critique group, NI—Rose Cooper, Ann Marie Meyers and Mindy Alyse Weiss—I couldn't survive another novel idea without you!

To my beta readers, T.P. Jagger and Niki Moss. Thank you for helping LDRH be all that it could! Words of thanks are never enough for readers who endure a first draft. There will be chocolate. I promise.

Thanks to my social networking buddies, writers, friends, and family far and wide for their witty quips and vampire puns. Erin R. Britt (bless her heart), Jenny Elliott, Angela Hartley, Shelley Rinehard , Roxanne Scheringer, and Aften Brook Szymanski . . . Scarlet wouldn't be nearly as punny without you.

My editor, McKelle George, for being such a joy to work with. Her genius ideas, superior skills, and patience brought LDRH to a whole. nother. level. Thank you!

Marissa Shields, my publicist, who deserves a round of applause (and cupcakes) for dealing with my wacky schedule.

Many thanks to the countless others involved in development of this book, from conception to publication.

Most of all, thanks to my husband and beautiful daughters for their continual support even when I didn't deserve it. You mean the world to me!

Amie

To my awesome B.A.B.E.s and my chill readers. Hope this book doesn't suck.

Bethanie

about the authors

AMIE BORST, a long-time writer and self-proclaimed graduate from ULE (University of Life Experience), is a native New Yorker, now residing in Northern Virginia. Originally, she aspired to be on Broadway, but her teen years were filled with too many "angsty" poems and short stories to let them fall to the wayside. She enjoys eating chocolate while writing and keeps a well-stocked stash hidden away from her family.

BETHANIE BORST is an all-rounder. She is a spunky 13-year-old who is an avid archer with Olympic dreams, enjoys the outdoors, loves reading and is quick to make lasting friendships. When she is not writing, she swings on a star.

Follow Amie and Bethanie on Facebook at:
facebook.com/AmieAndBethanieBorst

about the illustrator

RACHAEL CARINGELLA, also known as Rachael Tree Talker, got her name from talking to trees when she was little. Drawing inspiration from daydreams and nightmares, folklore and fantasy, she is fascinated by all things dark and dreary, morbid and macabre, balancing them with the playful, happy, and the beautiful. She loves creepy trees and big mysterious eyes that tell stories. Rachael lives in a little house in the forests of Utah working as a full time artist with a dog, a cat, a collection of creepy clown dolls, and vintage gumball machines. She has pink hair, and currently blogs at:

talk2thetrees.com